A NOTE TO DIE FOR

An Ami Dautry Mystery

Carol Rifon

CR Press   Cottonwood, Arizona

A NOTE TO DIE FOR
Copyright © 2023 by Carol Rifon

All rights reserved. No part of this book may be reproduced
or transmitted in any form or by any means without written
permission from the author.

ISBN-13 978-0-9841719-4-1
ISBN-10 0-9841719-4-0

Dedication

To my husband, Charles Riggio

Special Thanks
To Karen Hatler for her exceptional proofing abilities

Table of Contents

CHAPTER ONE

The Rehearsal

"Okay, everyone, we're about to begin our first off book. We expect lapses. Gregg will throw lines as needed," announced David Carson, the stage director. "Josh, all set with the vocal score?"

"Set!" replied Josh. Josh Boston was the musical director and wrote the score for this production. He was internationally known for his piano concerts and made considerable contributions to the Cypress Nest community for both theater productions and private charity events.

"Randall, I assume you'll be taking notes?"

"Yes," he answered. Randall Griffin was the librettist of this production, having written both the script and lyrics to be performed.

"Leo? Orchestra set?"

"Set!" replied Leo from the pit. As conductor of a nearby college orchestra, Leo Sullivan had arranged for his students to participate in the yearly Cypress Nest Community Theater production as part of their curriculum.

"When you're ready," directed David to Elise and Malcolm.

Elise Foster was an internationally known, retired soap star and frequent lead in the Cypress Nest Community Theater productions. She was one of the theater guild's chief financial contributors, second only to Sharon Hart Randall, a local philanthropist.

Malcolm Lawson was a recent retiree in Cypress Nest. Although not internationally known like Elise, he had been an actor for many years in bit parts in both film and television. Most importantly, he was a legit voice asset to the production.

Elise and Malcolm slowly walked downstage as they spoke their lines. Josh began playing the lead in. Elise and Malcolm began to sing to an upbeat tune.

>=<

"Any plans for this weekend, Ami?" asked Bill, as he and Ami sat having tea in the beautiful garden Bill had created at Cypress Cottage Bed and Breakfast.

Bill Arnold and Josh Boston owned the bed and breakfast. Ami had stayed there when she first moved to Cypress Nest over a year ago. Bill and Josh had become Ami's closest friends.

"Attending foreign film night. Bergman's *Wild Strawberries* is playing. I'm looking forward to it. I love foreign films. I know Josh will be busy with rehearsals, but would you like to join me?"

"Thank you, but I loathe subtitles and tend to get bored. You should ask Lucas. He's quite the foreign film buff."

Lucas Duncan was Cypress Nest's police chief. He and Ami initially met after a body had been found at the foot of her deck stairs shortly after she had moved to the community. She had been instrumental in helping him solve the case. They had an amicable relationship. He had escorted Ami to an art show and they had met socially at a number of local events over the past year. Although he had expressed interest in pursuing a relationship with her, Ami had halted further involvement due to still processing the death of her husband, George. Although the three-year anniversary of his death had passed, she felt reluctant to move on.

"I didn't know Lucas enjoyed foreign films. I suppose I could ask him."

Bill cocked his head. "Is it possible you are softening to the idea of dating him?"

"Lucas and I are casual friends. Friends can attend a film together without it being a date."

"You're blushing again, mon cher ami."

>=<

"Good start, everyone!" complimented David, as they concluded their first run. "Let's take ten."

The cast and crew quickly fled to the break room behind the stage.

David walked over to the production table. "Randall, comments?" he asked.

"Can we eliminate the third downstage turn in the second act? It blocks the flow of the song."

"Fine. Add it to the notes."

Josh got up from the piano and joined them.

"Comments, Josh?" asked David.

"I'd like to create a bridge for the ensemble singers at the end of act one. Let's split them with those stage left beginning, then joined by those stage right."

"Okay, we'll try it after break. Let's get a snack. My energy's beginning to dip," noted David.

They entered the break room to a chorus of laughter.

"What's the joke?" asked Randall.

"Kathy took a gulp of Justin's herbal coffee by mistake. The expression on her face was priceless!" giggled Sally Kirby, one of the singers.

"It was vile. I almost threw up," said Kathy Riggs, a fellow singer.

Justin Gibson refilled his cup and held it out to her. "Encore?"

She pushed it away. "No thanks!"

Nearby actors chuckled.

David smiled and reached for an apple.

>=<

"Okay, ensemble singers, let's take it from the bridge. Josh will play us in," directed David.

Josh began to play.

The ensemble singers, who were dispersed throughout the stage, joined in as instructed.

Suddenly, Justin Gibson extended his left arm, grab his chest with his right hand and fell to the floor, unconscious.

"Call 911!" yelled Kathy Riggs, running to assist him.

>=<

Ami and Bill looked up anxiously as Josh joined them at Off Broadway, the popular bistro across from the Cypress Nest Community Theater.

"Any word on Justin's condition?" asked Bill. "Shelby hasn't called me back. I've been frantic."

Josh flopped into the chair. "She spoke with David from the hospital. Justin suffered a massive heart attack."

"I don't understand why Shelby called David instead of me."

"She didn't. It was David who called her. The cast and crew were about to leave and anxious to hear. She asked him to let everyone else know."

"Well, she left me worried and waiting."

"My guess is she didn't call you back because she's trying to stay strong. She might break down if she talked to you," conjectured Josh.

"I suppose that's reasonable," grumbled Bill.

"There's more." Josh leaned toward Bill and lowered his voice. "They don't think Justin is going to make it. I'm so sorry." He placed his hand over Bill's.

"I'm sorry, Bill," said Ami. "I understand you were close friends."

"We were like brothers," softly answered Bill, a tear trickling down his face as he lowered his head.

Ami reached over and gently rubbed his shoulder.

Bill sat upright and shook his head. "No, a heart attack doesn't make sense. Justin keeps himself fit. I've never known him to have any kind of heart issues."

"Just because he never mentioned any doesn't mean he didn't have a problem," noted Josh.

"No," insisted Bill. "He would have told me."

"It's possible he was unaware of a heart condition. It's not uncommon for someone to have a heart attack from an unknown blockage," suggested Ami. "What about prescription medications? Is it possible his body reacted to a new medication?"

"Justin didn't take any medications. He took a few supplements, but that was it," said Bill.

"Supplements," repeated Josh. "You know, I overheard something when David called Shelby."

"What?" asked Bill and Ami in unison.

"When David was talking with Shelby, she asked him to hold on because one of the doctors was approaching her. He handed me the phone to wait for her while he informed the cast and crew of David's heart attack. I moved away from the group to wait for Shelby to come back to the phone. That's when I overheard the doctor talking to her. He said Justin's potassium level was unusually high and asked her if he was taking potassium supplements.

"Was he?" asked Ami.

"Shelby said she noticed a bottle on the kitchen counter and saw Justin slip it in his jacket pocket this morning."

Ami felt the hairs on her arms tingle. "Bill, did Justin mention taking potassium?"

"No. The only supplements he's ever mentioned taking were vitamin D and MSM/glucosamine. He'd have no reason to take potassium."

"They must think the high potassium is connected to his heart attack or they wouldn't have asked Shelby about it," proposed Ami. "At rehearsal, did Justin complain of feeling ill?"

"Not to me," said Josh, "but after the ambulance took him away, Kathy Riggs said that Justin mentioned his arms and legs feeling weak and dismissed it as too much yard work. And she noticed his arm shaking during break."

"Does that sound reasonable to you, Bill?" asked Ami.

"Being tired could be legitimate. Justin was an avid gardener and often overdid it, but the shaking sounds suspicious."

"Before you two go any further with your suppositions, let's order dinner," suggested Josh. "It's getting late and I have to go back to the theater to work on some changes for tomorrow." He sighed wearily and motioned for the waiter.

Ami noticed his eyes were sad and his body looked tense.

After they ordered, Ami turned to Josh. "It's too bad you have to go back to the theater. I'm sure you're tired and stressed by what happened today. I imagine the cast was very shaken."

"Everyone was frightened when it happened and still anxious after the ambulance left. The rest of rehearsal was awful. No one could concentrate. It would have been better if David had sent everyone home."

"I'm assuming the show will go on, as they say, but how do the actors and crew regroup after something like this?"

"It's challenging, but this isn't the first time we've had a medical emergency. Three years ago, our lead fell in the shower and slipped a disc. Luckily, his understudy proved very capable. Justin is an ensemble singer, so he's easier to replace from a production standpoint. We finished today's rehearsal with a swing. But Justin's loss is far more serious and possibly permanent. This hits us emotionally."

"Hopefully, he'll surprise the doctors and recover fully," offered Ami optimistically, although she didn't believe it for a minute. Instinctively, her gut told her Justin would die and it would be deemed homicide.

>=<

"Kathy, what are you still doing here?" asked Josh, returning to the theater to work on the revisions.

She was slumped on a chair, her arms dangling. She looked up at him. Her face was pale. "I felt too shaky to drive home." Her words were measured and slow.

"I'll be happy to drive you home," offered Josh. "Are you ill?"

"My arms and legs feel weak."

"You need to go to emergency immediately," ordered Josh. "No excuses. Come on," he said, helping her out of the chair.

>=<

"Ami, it's Bill. I called to fill you in on further developments. Josh took Kathy Riggs to the hospital. They found elevated levels of potassium in her system, too."

"Oh, this is more than coincidence. Is she okay?"

"Yes, thanks to Josh. He found her at the theater when he returned after our dinner. She told him her arms and legs felt weak. Josh made the connection with Justin's symptoms and took her straight to the ER."

"That was quick thinking on his part."

11

"Well, that's my Josh, le plus brilliant bulb in the lamp."

Ami smiled at Bill's bragging, but he was right. Josh was intelligent and, in this case, possibly had saved Kathy's life.

"Josh stayed with her for a couple hours," continued Bill. "He didn't want to leave her at the hospital alone. Kathy doesn't have any family here."

"That was kind of Josh."

"Well, you know how kind he is. Kathy's friend, Allison, arrived after she got off work, and she'll stay with her now."

"Are they keeping Kathy overnight?"

"I'm not sure. Josh and I have been communicating only by text so my information is limited," vented Bill with frustration.

"He'll fill you in on everything when he gets home. I'm sure he'll be there soon," soothed Ami.

"No, he won't. Josh has to go back to the theater to let the investigation team in."

"The police are involved already?"

"Josh called Lucas as soon as Kathy got her test results. Kathy insists she and Justin were poisoned. Lucas is taking her statement now."

"Do you know if anyone else at the theater got sick?"

"Josh started texting all of them as soon as he got to the hospital. So far, no one else is sick. We think it was specific to Justin and Kathy."

"I assume Justin is still too sick to provide any insight into this."

"He hasn't regained consciousness, yet. It may be a while before he'll be able to talk to the police."

Ami noticed the sadness in Bill's voice and a looming "if" in the air. She guessed, like her, he doubted Justin would regain consciousness.

In an attempt to shift the subject from Justin's condition, Ami noted, "The police must think it happened at rehearsal if they're checking the theater. I just hope they're able to find the evidence before whoever did this had a chance to remove it."

"This is much more sinister than we initially thought," declared Bill.

"Yes, it is. Looks like your suspicions at dinner tonight were right, Bill."

"I knew Justin didn't have a heart condition."

>=<

"Ms. Riggs, do you feel well enough to answer a few questions?" asked Chief Lucas Duncan.

"Yes," replied Kathy.

"I'd like to know about the food you ate at rehearsal today."

"I'm sure the potassium was in his coffee."

"Why do you say that?"

"Josh texted the others and no one else is sick. So, I've been thinking about what Justin and I both ate or drank that the others didn't and it was his coffee. The potassium had to be in there."

"Didn't others drink the coffee served at rehearsal?"

"Oh, I don't mean that coffee. Neither of us drank from the urn. Singers don't drink coffee. Caffeine is a no-no for us. Most of us bring a thermos of throat coat tea, but Justin preferred his special herbal coffee blend. He brought a thermos of that."

"Where was Mr. Gibson's thermos located?"

"Backstage. On the table with the others."

"And he shared it with you?"

"We weren't sharing it. I drank it by mistake. Our cups were side by side. I was busy talking to another cast member, picked up the wrong cup and took a big swallow.

13

It must have been loaded with potassium for that little bit to make me sick. I can only imagine how much Justin must have suffered before he collapsed." Her eyes filled with tears.

"Did the coffee taste bad, like something was in it?"

"It was bitter. Justin liked his bitter herbs so I didn't think anything of it at the time. But, since then, I've replayed it again and again in my mind. I'm pretty sure the coffee had a bit of a metallic taste, too."

"Do you have any idea who might want to hurt Mr. Gibson?"

"Of course. It was his wife, Shelby."

"Why would she want to do that?" asked Chief Duncan.

"For her freedom. Shelby was cheating on him. Sadly, we all knew it before Justin did. When he confronted her, she demanded an open marriage. Like she hadn't already insulted him enough! The cheating had hurt him deeply. He refused, of course, and asked for a divorce."

"How do you know all this?"

"Justin and I were close friends. He confided in me. Look, Justin asked for the divorce this past weekend. That's why I know it was her who poisoned him and, by extension, me. "

"The divorce would have allowed her to be free. Why poison him?"

"They had a prenup that would have made divorce very expensive for her. She didn't want to pay the money. That's her motive. And she had opportunity, too. Justin always prepared his herbal coffee first thing so it'd have time to steep while he dressed. Shelby poured it into his thermos so it'd be ready for him to take to rehearsal. It would have been easy for her to add potassium."

"Do you know what was in this herbal coffee of his?"

"Justin told me once. I know there was cinnamon.
That was the only ingredient I liked. He mentioned chicory
and dandelion and some other roots or seeds. Maybe
burdock? I can't remember. Justin had it written down on
a recipe card. I'm sure Shelby can give you the recipe,
minus the potassium, of course."

>=<

"Ami, it's Josh. I have some bad news."
"Is it about Justin?"
"Yes. He died last night."
"I'm so sorry. How is Bill?"
"He's heartbroken. I'm reluctant to leave him, but I
have to go to rehearsal. Do you think you could stop by
and keep him company?"
"Of course. My schedule is free today. I'll be over
right after breakfast."
"Thanks, Ami. I very much appreciate that."

>=<

"Okay, everyone, gather round," called David
Carson. "By now you've all heard the sad news of Justin's
passing. In addition, Kathy was taken ill."
The group quietly mumbled, but only Elise
interrupted David with a question.
"Is she okay? I heard Josh took her to emergency
last night."
"She's recovering nicely, but confined to home for
the next couple of days."
"Is it true they were poisoned?" asked Paul, one of
the supporting cast.
"Listen, it's understandable we all have questions,
but we've been asked to refrain from discussing this until
questioned by the police. As you are aware, they are here

15

and will be meeting with each of us privately. Karen has arranged for them to use the production office. I have promised full cooperation and that means accommodating them as necessary, even if it disrupts today's rehearsal. I realize this will be a difficult rehearsal for all of us, but it is necessary that we continue with our preparations for opening night. I suggest, as a way to focus and maintain our professionalism, we dedicate today's rehearsal as a respectful tribute to Justin. Okay, then, let's get on with it. Ensemble, I know you'll be thin, but we'll move forward with the revisions Josh made last night. Leo, I assume you have those?"

"Josh provided updated sheets," he answered.

"Randall, are you on board?"

"All set!" he called from the audience.

"When you're ready," directed David to Elise and Malcolm.

Elise and Malcolm slowly walked downstage as they spoke their lines. Josh began playing the lead in. Elise and Malcolm began to sing.

>=<

"Hi, Bill," said Ami, joining him in the garden of Cypress Cottage Bed and Breakfast. "I'm so sorry about Justin."

He looked up at her with puffy eyes. It was obvious he had been crying. "Thank you, mon cher ami."

She gave him a hug and sat down next to him.

"Can I get you anything?" offered Bill.

"No, I'm fine. My only interactions with Justin and Shelby were here and at a few club events, so I didn't know them well. Do they have children?"

"Justin does from a previous marriage. His son lives in L.A.; his daughter, in Washington state. I'm assuming Shelby called them and they're on their way."

"This will be a terrible shock for them. It's so sad," sympathized Ami.

"They'll take it hard. They loved their father. Justin's death is heartbreaking for all of us. He was well loved."

"Bill, when Josh came home last night, did he mention if the police found any evidence at the theater?"

"He didn't stay there. He let them in, left his key with Lucas to lock up, and drove home. He was exhausted. I'm sorry I don't know more."

"It doesn't matter. I doubt they would have shared that information with him anyway," dismissed Ami.

"The question that haunts me is who would do this to Justin. He's always been easy going and pleasant. No grudges. No enemies."

"It's often a spouse that does this sort of thing. Do you think it's possible that Shelby could be involved?"

"I can't imagine Shelby doing something like this, although their marriage had been rocky lately," admitted Bill.

"By rocky, do you mean affairs?"

"Yes. Although Justin did his best to pamper her, Shelby seemed unhappy in their relationship. Personally, I think she was bored with him. Shelby can be immature and self centered, but she's not evil. I can't believe she would have killed him."

"What about business dealings or financial problems? Did he seem upset recently?"

"Nothing like that. Justin was wise with his money."

"What about his family? Did he seem troubled about anything connected with his children?"

"No. His children are independent and successful. His relationship with them has always been a loving one, although a bit strained over the past year. They did not approve of his marriage to Shelby."

"Which means, had they been involved, they would have poisoned her, not him," suggested Ami.

"Exactly. I can't think of any reason for anyone to hurt him."

"So, you're saying that other than his rocky relationship with Shelby, everything else was smooth?"

"Yes. That seemed his only concern."

>=<

"Mr. Griffin, I'd like you to describe what you witnessed yesterday regarding Mr. Gibson's health and ultimate collapse."

"Really, Lucas? Don't you think we know each other well enough to drop the formality?"

Lucas glanced over at the officer beside him recording the interview and nodded. He turned back to Randall Griffin. "Tell me what you know, Randall."

"I know there was something physically wrong with Justin. I noticed it myself."

"What did you notice?"

"After morning break, he was lethargic. He's usually alert and energized. Following afternoon break, he was almost stumbling around the stage. I'm guessing it was the afternoon dose of poison that got him. I think I can provide a timeline for you."

"You heard he was poisoned?"

"Come on, Lucas. You know what gossip is like around here. It was all over town by last night."

"Tell me about the timeline."

"I think it happened at three yesterday afternoon. That was just about the time David, Josh and I walked into the break room."

"Describe what happened."

"As we walked in, the group near Justin was laughing and teasing Kathy. She had taken a big swallow of his herbal coffee by mistake. It made her cough and almost hurl. I remember seeing Justin refill his cup from his thermos and hold it out to Kathy, teasing her with more. I noticed his arm and hand were shaking. She refused, of course. Good thing she did or she'd be dead now, too. Break was almost over, so he downed the contents himself and the cast went back on stage. It would have been easy for somebody to have slipped something into his thermos."

"Did you notice anyone back stage that wasn't part of the cast or crew?"

"No. Means it must have been one of us who killed him. That's a sad and scary thought."

"So far, this appears specific to Justin. I don't believe the cast and crew need to be frightened."

"That's not what I meant. This is a supportive theater group. Believe me, they're not all like this. Worked in some that were pretty cut throat. Not to say we don't have our egos, but David knows how to keep them in check. Hate to see that trust broken."

"I'm sure you do. I'd like you to tell me more about Justin stumbling on stage before he collapsed."

"I noted it here." He opened his notepad and held it out to Lucas.

Lucas quietly read the notes. "Can you send me this file?"

"Sure. Why don't you just go ahead and send it to yourself right now?"

Lucas did so.

"I guess you'll want a copy of the video, too," said Randall.

"There's video? No one mentioned you recorded rehearsals?"

"I usually don't bother until we get closer to dress, but Josh and I discussed better coordinating the music to movement and thought a recording would help. Let me pull up the file for you." Randall took the notepad from

Lucas and made a few entries. "Okay, I sent it to you." He held out the notepad. "Want to look at it now? Warning, it runs over two hours."

"No, I'll check it later and get back to you with any questions. Any recording equipment in the break room?"

"No reason to record there."

"Randall, are you aware of Justin arguing or having disagreements with anyone in the last couple weeks?"

"I didn't hear of any. Sounds unlikely though. He was an even-tempered guy."

"What about jealousy toward him from other cast members?"

"Not that I'm aware of. Anyway, there'd be no reason. His role was supporting. He was understudying for Malcolm, but he wasn't threatening anybody's spotlight."

"Anything else you think I ought to know?"

"I'd note the part of the recording just prior to Justin collapsing. You'll see three people focused on Justin just before it happened. Direction is to focus on the lead actors, so it strikes me curious as to why they were focused on Justin."

"You're very observant, Randall," complimented Lucas.

Randall nodded. "Credit years of assessing the movements of actors."

"Thanks for the specific and detailed information. Too bad you're not a witness in all my investigations."

"No offense, but I regret being involved in this one."

CHAPTER TWO

The Surprise

"Hi, Aunt Ami!"

"Marianne! How nice to hear from you." Ami loved her niece, not only as her older sister's daughter, but as a dear friend. Despite the almost thirty year age difference, their relationship was that of confidants.

"I'm in Monterey with Granny and wondered if you had time in your schedule tomorrow to drive over. I have a surprise to share with you."

Monterey was about an hour's drive from Cypress Nest where Ami lived.

"Sure, Dear, I can join you tomorrow," happily agreed Ami.

"Great! Be at Granny's at noon and I'll take you to the surprise and then I'll treat you both to lunch."

"I'm looking forward to it."

>=<

"Ta-da!" announced Marianne, pulling into the driveway of a large and impressive home. "It's mine. I bought it. Well, Mike and I bought it."

"Oh, this is very grand," declared Granny, known as Claire Martin to those other than her grandchildren.

"It's huge. I'm thrilled for you and Mike," cheered Ami. "But why didn't you tell us you were moving to Monterey?"

"I wanted it to be a surprise. Surprise! Come on," ordered Marianne, opening the car door. "You have to see it!"

Ami and Claire removed themselves from the car and followed Marianne up the walkway to the front door.

"We were really torn between this hilltop one and a smaller one right on the beach. Mike liked this view better. I liked that it was more modern. Bonus is, it's move-in ready," prattled Marianne, unlocking the door. "Wait til you see the ocean view. It's fantastic!"

>=<

"I came to talk to you about Justin's murder," stated Bill.

"Certainly, Bill, have a seat," invited Lucas.

Bill pulled out a chair and sat down. "First off, I'm here to provide any information that you think can help catch the person who did this. Justin was a wonderful man and I want his killer held accountable. I don't want this to be one of those unsolved murders."

"I promise I won't let that happen."

"Thank you. I want to state straight out that Justin did not have a heart condition and he didn't take potassium supplements, so there's no chance of this being anything but murder. Someone deliberately put potassium in his coffee. And since Kathy drank some by mistake, I think he was the only intended victim."

"Any idea who or why?"

"That's the problem. I can't think of a reason. Justin would have told me if he was in any kind of trouble. We were like brothers."

"What about his marriage?"

"Well, everyone knew Shelby was cheating on him. Justin told me he had seen his attorney and planned to file for divorce. He swore me to secrecy and I kept my promise. As you can imagine, it was killing me not to tell."

Lucas nodded, fully understanding Bill's weakness for gossip.

"This past weekend, he told Shelby about the divorce."

"How did she take it?" asked Lucas.

"Balked at divorce. He said she tried to convince him to agree to an open marriage."

"And?" prodded Lucas.

"Oh, he was too conventional for anything like that. He told her it was over and he was moving forward with the divorce."

"Do you think she killed him?"

"I honestly can't imagine she'd do that. Problem is, I can't think of anyone else who had a motive."

>=<

"So, like me, you decided to move from east to west coast. What prompted the big move?" asked Ami, as she, Marianne and Claire sat having lunch.

"I wanted to be closer to you and Granny. I really miss you, Aunt Ami!"

"I miss you, too, Dear."

"I suppose it helps that it's miles away from your mother," teased Claire.

"Well, that's a bonus," giggled Marianne. "I love her, but you know how she is."

"Intimately," moaned Claire. "She's been a control freak since birth. No idea why. Certainly not in mine or your father's genes."

"I've always suspected the hospital switched babies on you," suggested Ami with a smile.

"Of course, that must be the answer." Claire wrinkled her nose. "Too late to return her, I suppose."

Marianne laughed.

"All kidding aside," said Ami, "your moving closer to us has to be hard for her. How's she taking it?"

"As a personal insult. Dad was supportive, as usual."

Ami was not surprised at her sister, Suzi's, response. Suzi resented Marianne's closeness with her aunt and grandmother. She bristled at Marianne's free spirit, especially since it so closely mimicked her grandmother's. Of course, the family irony was that Ami's daughter, Shirley, was as controlling as Suzi.

"She'll change her tune when she sees your luxurious home. You know how impressed she is with grandeur," reminded Claire.

"That's true, but I expect a lecture on the dangers of extravagance and debt."

"Surely, she's aware you can afford it." Ami estimated Marianne's monthly income from her creation of a video game called TriangleTarget exceeded her parents' yearly salaries.

"She dismisses my work as playing video games. She sees Mike as our sole provider."

"So she has no idea how much money you make?"

"No. I figure the less she knows, the less advice she can give me. And, as you know, to her, advice means control. Speaking of control, I'm sorry Shirley isn't letting Teddy come for his summer visit again this year."

"Why not?" asked Claire.

"She's using the excuse we live close enough, now that I'm on the west coast, to visit each other any time, but it's really her way of punishing me for not moving in with them."

After Ami's husband, George, died, Shirley insisted Ami move to Oregon and live with her family. Ami's refusal, and her subsequent move to Cypress Nest, angered Shirley.

"She doesn't take rejection well, does she? I'm sorry she's hurting you, Darling."

"Thanks, Mom. The upside is, Teddy and I text often, so at least I get to keep in touch with him."

"It's odd that two open-minded women like ourselves have such repressed daughters," noted Claire.

"Are you implying we were bad mothers?"

"Of course, not. I'm complaining we have bad daughters." Claire laughed joyfully.

"It's because of fear. That's what's behind their controlling behavior. Basic psychology," diagnosed Marianne.

Ami smiled at the psychology course analysis. Much like her grandmother, Marianne enjoyed taking courses. She would submerge herself in a subject, inflict that information on everyone around her and then capriciously drop it for a new interest. Mike was the constant in Marianne's life. They had been married for seven years.

"Well, let's change the subject back to your exciting news," suggested Ami. "I wish you and Mike many years of happiness in your beautiful new home. I can't get over the size of it. I think my whole house could fit in your living room."

"It's an enormous living room," agreed Claire. "And that sectional is impressive."

"Don't you just love it! It's my first furniture in my new house. At first, I wasn't sure about it. I mean three, seven-foot sofa pieces seemed a lot, but Bill said we had to have it. He ordered it for me and, yesterday, when it was delivered, I was so excited, I had to bite my tongue not to spill it all to you, Granny."

"I expect you and Bill will have a great time working on the house together," said Ami.

In addition to running the Cypress Nest Bed and Breakfast and designing his beautiful garden, Bill was a retired interior designer who had helped, and expertly directed, Marianne's feng shui of Ami's home. Feng shui having been another of Marianne's courses. Bill and

Marianne had become fast friends due to their mutual interests. Both were over six foot tall and loved to gossip.

"Bill's coming to see it next week. I gave him a video tour and had to threaten him with bodily harm to keep this move a secret. You know what a gossip he is."

"You can be proud of him. Not even a hint to me."

"We're planning a shopping trip to LA to buy all new stuff. Mike and I sold all the furniture in our other houses so we'd have little to ship out. Mike's thrilled Bill is helping me. He's not the least bit interested in picking out wall colors or furniture."

"So, what about Mike? I know you can work from anywhere. Is he getting a transfer?" asked Ami.

"Mike quit. He's been working sixty hours a week and really needed a break. So, he's decided to work on his own as a consultant. He's really looking forward to his freedom."

"Good for him! I'm so pleased," congratulated Claire, who, currently in her seventies and retired, had enjoyed her freedom as a freelance travel photographer. She had toured the world a few times over and, although it took a toll on her marriage, never regretted it. After many years of living separate lives, she finally divorced Ami's and Suzi's father. She continued to enjoy her freedom by never remarrying.

"This is a scary big move for us, but I know it's right because things are going along so smoothly and quickly, you know?"

"Yes, Darling, I do know. Things move quicker when you flow along with the current."

"That's exactly what's happening, Granny! Last month, we sold our house in Wilmington and this month, the house in Seashell Beach. Last week, we closed on this one. And in five weeks, Mike will be out and we'll be moved in. It's all flowing along like it was meant to be."

Ami had been watching Marianne's face as she talked. As a portrait artist, she had studied and painted faces for years and could read emotions, even those deeply hidden, particularly within the eyes. Marianne's eyes were animated and filled with joy, which was not unusual for Marianne, but there was an extra special sparkle there.

"And I have a feeling you have another surprise to tell us, Dear."

Marianne's eyes widened. "I thought only Granny was clairvoyant."

"Your eyes gave you away. They're sparkling more than usual. So, what's your other surprise?"

"I'm pregnant!" blurted Marianne.

"I'm so happy for you!" Ami and Claire shouted simultaneously.

"Thanks. Mike and I are thrilled. I'm barely pregnant so we planned to wait until I was further along before announcing it. We haven't even told our parents."

"A grandchild should make your mother happy," noted Claire.

"I know. Luckily, we'll be too far away for her to drop by and try to take over." Marianne grinned broadly. "We've been trying for over a year and nothing happened. So, we decided to take a break from making a baby and make this move instead. Then, bam! Suddenly I was pregnant. That's the main reason I'm happy everything is rolling along so quickly. We'll be moved in and settled long before the baby comes. I can't wait to start decorating the nursery. It will be all soft colors and gentle energy."

"I can confirm your new house has great energy. I recently completed a course in environmental mindfulness and I felt clear vibrations throughout it," advised Claire.

"Ooh, how wonderful! Environmental mindfulness sounds so interesting. Tell me about it."

"Not now, Marianne. It's too involved. Let's save this discussion until we have lots of time to explore it."

"We'll have plenty of time for long visits now that I'll be living close to you."

"I'm happy about that, too, Darling, but no dropping in. Call first. And don't expect me to babysit," warned Claire. "My calendar is filled to the brim with academic, political and social commitments."

Marianne smiled, "I promise not to impose."

>=<

"Thanks for having me to dinner," said Lucas.

"Our pleasure. I've been so busy with the musical, I feel we've neglected our friendship," replied Josh, filling the wine glasses.

"Not at all," assured Lucas.

"Josh made me promise no shop talk tonight, even though I'm curious about how your investigation is going. Any quick hints before dinner?"

"No, Bill," insisted Josh. "We all need a night of relaxation and friendship."

"I'm for that," toasted Lucas, raising his glass, and then taking a sip of wine.

"Well, since we're keeping this friendly and personal. I think Ami is softening toward you, Lucas," disclosed Bill.

"What do you mean?"

"She's into foreign films and asked me to go with her this weekend."

Josh laughed. "You?"

"I know. I told her I hated them. I wouldn't last fifteen minutes."

"Less than five," interjected Josh.

Bill ignored Josh and turned to Lucas. "I mentioned that you loved them. To my surprise, she said she might call and ask you to go with her."

"I won't hold my breath," dismissed Lucas.

"But you'd go, wouldn't you?" urged Bill.

"Of course. I'm just not counting on it."

"If only she'd lay George to rest. I truly believe she cares for you," insisted Josh.

"Well, my advice is to hang in there. I know you've been waiting for over a year now, but I've got an inkling she's getting close," assured Bill. "Please promise me you'll wait a little longer."

"I'm a patient man," replied Lucas.

>=<

At Marianne's cajoling and bribing them with in-home massages provided by the local spa, Ami and Claire agreed to a slumber party at Marianne's new house.

As they each lounged on one of the huge sectional sofas in their spa robes, another gift from Marianne, enjoying their post massage euphoria, they sipped lemon flavored sparkling water.

"Just think, Marianne. Soon, you'll bring a beautiful new baby into this beautiful new home. I'm happy for you," proclaimed Claire.

"I feel really happy, too. And really grateful. I appreciate how fortunate we are."

"All of this is grand, Darling, but your greatest blessing is that abundance of love in your life."

"I agree. Love is what really matters in life," said Ami.

"That's not what Bill says you think," countered Marianne. "You know he keeps me informed about your love life or lack thereof."

"What are you talking about?"

"According to Bill, you're blocking love from your life."

"What love?"

"Lucas, of course! He said even though you refuse to date Lucas, you turn bright red whenever he's around or his name comes up. We both think your blushing means your body wants him, but you won't allow yourself to indulge."

"I don't blush about Lucas. I have occasional hot flashes."

"I think you're flashing hot for Lucas! Bill said Lucas has been waiting for you to let go of Uncle George, but he's not going to wait forever. If you honestly believe love is what really matters, you ought to consider that."

"I'd like to hear more about Lucas," said Claire.

"Ooh, he's perfect for her," offered Marianne. "Bill and I watched them dance together at Nancy's party and when they smiled at one another, there was definitely a spark."

"What are his interests?"

"He's Cypress Nest's police chief. Aunt Ami helped him last year with two murders, one was right at the steps of her new house!"

"Sounds exciting, Marianne, but I was asking Ami. You never mentioned a murder, Ami. Why not?"

"It was over a year ago, Mom. I was busy with the new house and assumed Marianne had told you all about it. She was there at the time."

"Yes, it was thrilling! One of the killers threatened Aunt Ami with a knife and I knocked her out with a kick. Anyway, I could tell right away Lucas was into Aunt Ami. I tried my best at matchmaking, but she wasn't having it. Lucas said he finds her mind intriguing. I like his mind, too. He's quick and good at verbal sparring. And he's nice looking, too, you know, for an older guy. He's big, strong, keeps himself fit. Most women Aunt Ami's age would consider him a catch."

"He sounds like an interesting person. Ami, what's your opinion of Lucas?"

"I consider him intelligent and kind."

"How do you feel about his attraction to you?" nudged Claire.

"It's flattering, but I'm not interested in a relationship. I made that clear to him."

"If you made it clear, why do you think he continues to wait for you?"

"He's not waiting for me."

"Bill said he is," inserted Marianne.

"Ami?" Claire took a sip and water and stared at her daughter.

"I have no idea why he'd wait."

"It stands to reason he'd only wait if you were sending him signals he has a chance."

"I'm not sending him any signals."

"Ooh, look at you! You're blushing just talking about him!" shouted Marianne.

"I'm having a hot flash."

"You are not! You're attracted to him!"

"Marianne, stop pushing this," ordered Ami.

"I'm curious as to why you're denying your obvious attraction to Lucas," confronted Claire.

"This conversation is uncomfortable."

Claire smiled. "Good."

"Look, I don't want to discuss this."

"But I do," insisted Claire, in a tone that meant she wasn't giving up.

"Uh oh," murmured Marianne.

Claire shot her granddaughter a quieting stare, then turned to Ami. "Marianne's right about your blushing. Your body has feelings for Lucas and you need to address them."

"Yes!" emphasized Marianne, raising her hands in the air.

"Marianne, allow me to continue without comment," instructed Claire.

Marianne pulled her fingers over her lips in a closed zipper motion.

"Ami, love is a precious gift. You were fortunate to have it with George. And now love is presenting itself again. Why are you refusing this gift?"

"Because what I had with George can't be repeated."

"Why would you want to repeat what you've already lived? Lucas is a new adventure. Oh, I know a new relationship is fraught with fears, but it also can be exciting and satisfying. Surely it can't hurt to jump in and swim around a little. Why not allow yourself to test the waters?"

"But what about George?"

"Darling, George has been dead for three years. You're still alive. Denying yourself love is not a tribute to him. He doesn't want that kind of sacrifice from you. Your mind may be holding on to him, but your body is telling you that it's time to let go."

"You surprise me, Mom. In my whole life, I can't remember you ever giving me advice like this."

"Your life was yours to live and you were happy with your choices. I'm speaking now because I see you hiding in the past and denying yourself an opportunity for happiness. Those of us who are alive have a responsibility to live life fully. I hope you will allow yourself to do that."

>=<

"Hi, Lucas, it's Ami."

"Hello, Ami. What can I do for you?"

"Bill said you enjoy foreign films. Bergman's *Wild Strawberries* is playing. I have tickets for Friday night. Would you like to go with me?"

"I'd love to," he replied.

"Also, I enjoy talking about films as much as seeing them. How about we go to the early show and have coffee or a drink afterwards?" she suggested.

"Sounds great!"

"Wonderful. I'll pick you up at six."

>=<

"It looks more beautiful every time I see it," expressed Roselyn Kelly, studying her portrait.

"I'm pleased you like it," said Ami. "Are there any changes you'd like me to make?"

"No. Please continue as is."

"Okay then, have a seat. This won't take long. I just want to fine tune your facial features. Now, lift your head just a bit and look over my right shoulder," directed Ami. "Perfect!" She studied Roselyn's face. "I sense something wrong, Roselyn. There's a sadness in your eyes."

"I was just thinking about Shelby. I'm sure you've heard about Justin."

"Yes. His passing is very sad," sympathized Ami. "Would you like to stop and continue another day?"

"I'd like to stay if it won't affect the portrait."

"It won't. And please feel free to talk. It will help you release those emotions."

"It's just that I'm concerned about Shelby. She seems frightened. Although she hasn't said it, I'm wondering if she's worried someone might kill her, too."

"Justin's killer hasn't been arrested yet. I suppose that could make her feel vulnerable and afraid. Also, she's grieving the loss of her husband. That's a lot to deal with."

"In addition, Justin's children arrived last night. She's uncomfortable around them. Finds it very stressful. You see, they've never accepted her. They didn't approve of their father marrying someone like her."

"Someone like her?"

"Someone much younger than him and sexy. They view her as a gold digger."

Ami raised her eyebrows.

"Not the case," assured Roselyn. "Shelby's worth way more than Justin. Huge inheritance. Point is, his children have always been angry about it. They've chosen to stay with Bill rather than at the house with Shelby."

"I imagine that hurt Shelby's feelings."

"Shelby said she's relieved she doesn't have to deal with them. I can see her point, but I guess I'd prefer to see them all supporting one another like a family. I feel sorry for his kids. No matter their view of Shelby, they loved their father. His death has to be a great loss for them."

"Maybe giving one another space is a positive thing. Justin's death occurred suddenly. That kind of shock and confusion can be overwhelming. And it makes sense they'd want to stay with Bill. He was their father's closest friend and they've known him for many years. I'm sure he'll be of great comfort to them."

"That seems logical. And you're right about Bill. He would be much more comforting than Shelby."

"All done," announced Ami, putting down her brush. "Come take a look."

Roselyn got up and joined Ami at the easel. She slowly scanned the painting, then turned to Ami. "It's perfect," she said, smiling the same smile as in the portrait.

CHAPTER THREE

The Proposition

"Even though I've seen this film several times, I continue to be awed by the recurring theme of guilt in the dream sequences," asserted Lucas.

"Most chilling to me is that visit to his mother. That explains the guilt," offered Ami.

"I'm enjoying this. I've been unable to interest any of my friends in foreign films. Josh and Bill were a firm no. Finally convinced Arthur to join me, but I could tell he didn't enjoy it. I'm glad you do though. Now, I have someone to appreciate them with. How did you get interested?"

"My mother. She and I used to go about once a month. She loved Bergman. *Fanny and Alexander* was her favorite. How about you?"

"I grew up in LA where my mother produces independent films and my father's an entertainment attorney. Both retired, for the most part. Huge film buffs. They took me to see Clouzot's *The Wages of Fear* when I was fourteen. That hooked me."

"I guess we should thank our parents for providing us with a love for great films."

"We should," agreed Lucas, raising his coffee cup in toast. "You know, throughout the evening, I've had the feeling you had something on your mind. Do you want to tell me what it is?"

"Oh, you noticed. Well, I just wanted to ask you…I mean," stammered Ami, blushing. She shook her head. "Never mind. Let's talk about Justin Gibson's death."

"What about it?"

"It was murder. An overdose of potassium. Justin was deliberately poisoned and Kathy accidentally," summarized Ami.

"And what brings you to this conclusion?"

"The rumors are all over town."

Lucas raised an eyebrow. "I expected something more logical from you than rumors."

"There's often logic at the bottom of rumors. More importantly is Bill's take on it. The minute Josh told him about the heart attack, Bill wasn't buying it. He said Justin did not have heart issues."

"Go on," urged Lucas.

"Josh mentioned he overheard the doctors question the high level of potassium in Justin's body and then Kathy had high potassium levels, too, with the same, but milder, symptoms. A quick online research of potassium overdose included those symptoms and said an overdose can cause a heart attack. Bill said the potassium was in Justin's herbal coffee that Justin and Kathy consumed at rehearsal."

"And do you have a suspect?" asked Lucas.

"His wife, Shelby. Bill mentioned Shelby and Justin's marriage was rocky because Shelby had an affair or maybe more than one."

"So, your theory is she wanted out and killed him?"

"Possibly. Bill told me that Shelby asked for an open marriage, but Justin wouldn't go along with it."

"There's always divorce."

"What if Justin refused to give her a divorce? What if she was in love with another man and wanted to remarry? What if, in her desire to be free, she decided to kill Justin? What if she chose potassium supplements because they're easy to buy at the store? What if she thought the potassium in his body wouldn't be recognized as a poison because it's a supplement? What if she had been lacing his food with potassium for months and this final dose was the one that killed him?"

"That's a lot of what ifs," stated Lucas.

"Can you tell me if the medical examiner confirmed Justin's death was due to a potassium overdose?"

Lucas smiled. "Since the whole town seems to know and the report will be publicly released tomorrow morning, I'll tell you. Yes. It's a homicide."

"And do you suspect Shelby?" nudged Ami.

"You know I won't discuss case details."

"When Roselyn Kelly came over today for a final sitting, she mentioned that Justin's kids disliked Shelby. They thought she was a gold digger and disapproved of their father marrying her. So much so, that they are staying with Bill rather than at their father's house with Shelby. Roselyn said Shelby was better off financially than Justin, so the gold digger part wasn't true, but I wondered if his kids were worried about her getting their inheritance."

"And?"

"And so I asked Sharon to make a few calls. She found out that all of Justin's money goes directly to his kids. Plus, Sharon confirmed Shelby's wealth. It's from a family inheritance and it's a bundle. I know that rules out Justin's money as a motive for Shelby, but she still had the motive of wanting an open marriage. And, as his wife, she had easy access to his food. That gives her motive and opportunity."

"You've been a busy bee," assessed Lucas. "Seems to me you have an unusually keen interest in this."

"Well, I'm angry that Justin had his life cut short. It's unfair. Mostly, I'm sad for Bill. This is a great loss for him. He wants to know who did this and wants them held accountable. So do I."

"And so do I. That's what investigations help determine. If I give you points for your investigative skills, do you think we can agree to shelve the shop talk and get back to discussing films?" suggested Lucas.

"Of course, you need a break from work. I was so focused on my theories, I didn't consider it from your end."

"It's okay." Lucas studied her for a minute. "Your expression tells me there's something else on your mind. Do you have another point you'd like to make?"

"It's not about Justin."

"Well, what is it?"

Ami blushed. "There's something else I've been wanting to ask you all night. It's what I really wanted to ask earlier, but I don't have any experience doing this sort of thing. I'm not sure how to start."

"Really? Can't imagine you being at a loss for words."

She frowned at him.

"Okay. No jokes. You have my full attention."

"Now, I'm feeling foolish and embarrassed. Didn't expect to be this nervous."

"When I'm nervous about saying something, I find it helps to just go for it. Try blurting out the first few words and see where it takes you," he advised.

Ami sighed. "Okay." She closed her eyes and announced, "I find you intelligent, kind and appealing." She opened them and looked at his face as she continued, "I'm attracted to you and would like to have a relationship with you."

He grinned broadly, but didn't speak.

"Well? Are you interested?"

"Yes! I'm delighted."

She studied his face. "You're telling the truth. I can see it in your eyes."

"Of course I am. If you'll recall, I stated a while ago that I wanted to be with you, but I've been respecting your boundaries, as promised. What about your late husband?"

"I know this is going to sound like I'm some kind of kook, but I talked it over with George and he told me to let him rest in peace and to move on with my life."

"I don't consider you a kook. I'm happy you feel resolved to move on with your life. And grateful you're including me in it. It's what I've been hoping for."

Ami smiled. "I have to admit I'm relieved at your response. I was afraid sharing my feelings so openly and honestly would turn you off."

"Exact opposite. I appreciate honesty. I'm not interested in playing games. Although I have to confess I attended a number of those club events just so I could dance with you. It was during those dances that you let your guard down just a little bit and connected with me."

"I guess it's because I feel free when dancing. I love to dance."

Lucas smiled. "Well, tomorrow night, there's a dinner dance at the club. Would you like to go with me?"

"I'd love to, but I already promised Bill I'd go with him. Josh is busy with his music."

"I'll call Bill and ask if I can join the two of you. I'm sure he wouldn't mind. Would you be okay with that?"

"Yes, I'd like that."

>=<

"Last night, the film. Tonight, another date," remarked Bill, twirling Ami around the dance floor. "May I assume you're a couple now?"

"Too soon, Bill," cautioned Ami.

"I've been hoping you'd get together and I'm anxious for confirmation."

"I promise if Lucas and I become a couple, you'll be the first person we tell. Okay?"

"I await the news, mon cher ami."

>=<

It was late in the evening and most of the group had left the dance. Club waiters circled small tables, serving coffee to the few remaining couples.

Lucas stared at Ami and smiled.

"What is it?"

"I'm feeling happy," said Lucas. "Tonight, for the first time, you were present and connected with me. I've been wanting that and now I'm happy."

"I'm happy, too. It felt good to let my defenses down and just have fun." She had more than enjoyed dancing with Lucas tonight. She had felt thrilled and excited, almost giddy. "It seems my mother was right."

"About what?"

"She told me you cared or you wouldn't be waiting for me. She told me I had feelings for you, too. She told me to live life to the fullest."

"I'm grateful to your mother. And I more than care for you, I love you. I'm sure of it, but, then, I'm a year ahead of you in this relationship." He leaned back in his chair as he continued. "I don't expect you to say it back. And I don't intend to rush you. We'll move forward at whatever pace you find comfortable. Ami, I'm taking this seriously. Are you?"

"Up until this point, my entire life has consisted of one relationship. I took that very seriously. I don't think I'd know how to be casual about love. And I feel love for you, too. I have for a while now."

"I'm pleased to hear that," he replied, reaching over and clasping her hand. "This is a beginning for us."

Their eyes locked and Ami was ignited with a passion so intense she felt she might burst into flames. She smiled and slowly eased her hand from his. She leaned back in her chair and let out a long soft sigh. After a moment, she leaned forward. "I'd like to ask you a rather personal question."

"Ask me anything," he encouraged.

"Would you be interested in having sex?"

Lucas widened his eyes and stared at her. Then, a grin slowly brightened his face. "Not many people surprise me. You totally disarmed me. I continue to find you a very intriguing woman."

>=<

"Do I smell pancakes?" asked Ami, walking into Lucas' kitchen. "They smell wonderful."

"I sense surprise."

"Maybe a little. I connect you with crime, not cooking."

"I'll have you know I'm a good cook. Nothing gourmet, but tasty." Lucas pulled the last pancake off the griddle and flipped it onto the plate. "Need to eat them while they're hot. Syrup and coffee are on the table."

Ami followed him to the dining room.

He placed a plate in front of her. "Dig in."

Ami took a bite. "These are really good."

"Thanks," replied Lucas. "Let's get married."

"What? Lucas, we don't know each other well enough."

He tilted his head. "I'd hardly say that."

She tilted her head in like fashion. "Really? Be serious."

"I am." He put down his fork and stared at her. "You know as well as I do that we've been in an undeclared relationship since that first dance at Sharon's party over a year ago. Finally, we've made this open and amazing connection. Why shouldn't we maintain this? I want us to be together."

"I feel the connection, too, and, you're right, it is amazing," agreed Ami.

41

"So, what's the point of going back to living in separate corners? I want to come home to you at night and wake up with you in the morning."

"I have to admit the thought of leaving you makes me sad."

"So don't."

"My mind keeps saying this is happening way too fast, but it doesn't feel reckless. I feel perfectly safe and comfortable."

"That's because we're mature and sensible people who know the difference between love and infatuation."

"The cautious part of me wants to come up with an objection, but I don't have one."

"Then, let's get married," he restated.

"I suppose there are daily flights from Monterey to Las Vegas," suggested Ami.

>=<

"Ami, what a surprise!"

"Hi, Mom. This is Lucas."

"Aah, Lucas." She gave him a wide smile. "It's a pleasure to meet you." She turned to Ami. "Darling, you should have called first. I don't have time for a visit. My drone group is picking me up in a few minutes. It's my latest passion." She stopped speaking and studied them. "Ooh, I see you don't have time for a visit either. Flying off to Vegas to get married, are you?"

"How?" Ami managed before her mother cut her off.

"Oh, please, the two of you are blasting the room with sexual energy. Your auras are flashing bright pink light and your double heartbeat of sincerity is pumping loudly in my ears."

"What?" asked Lucas.

"I took a course in clairvoyance once. Turns out, I had the gift, but that's another story," she dismissed. "I assume you're here because you need me to act as a buffer. No doubt about it, your daughter will have an apoplectic fit when you tell her. Don't worry about Shirley, I promise to defend you to the death."

Ami smiled. "Suzi always said you were witchy wise."

"No, Darling, your sister called me a witch. I added the wise. She'll disapprove, as well. Personally, I'm thrilled for you! And you're smart to move swiftly. You're too old to dilly dally around. Much happiness!" She kissed Ami's cheek. "Welcome to the family, Lucas," she said, kissing his cheek, too. "Okay, let's get going," she ordered, opening the front door. She ushered them outside and locked the door. "Come back soon for a long visit. Next time, call first." She hurried to the street and got into a waiting SUV filled with what appeared to be college-aged youth.

Lucas shook his head and turned to Ami. "Your mother is Marianne, fifty years in the future."

Amy chuckled. "Personality wise, Marianne is my mother's mini-me."

"I can see a lot of your mother in you, too, now that you've let your guard down."

"I am enjoying feeling open and free again."

"I gather your daughter and sister are critical of this free style that you, your mother and Marianne share?"

"I'm afraid so. My daughter will not approve of our marriage. And my sister will side with her."

"Should I prepare to be snubbed?"

"Much worse. They'll reject us both."

"I'm sure that will be painful for you. Are you having second thoughts?"

"Not a chance."

"Ami, thanks for inviting us to dinner," greeted Josh, giving her a hug at the door.

"Hello, mon cher ami," greeted Bill, kissing Ami on both cheeks.

As Josh walked into the living room, his face filled with surprise at seeing Lucas. "Hello, Lucas, this is an unexpected pleasure."

Ami hurried over to Lucas and stood beside him.

"I sense something is afoot. Tell me immediately," demanded Bill.

Ami and Lucas held up their left hands and flashed their wedding bands.

Bill dropped open his mouth and gasped. Then, he yelled, "I'm shocked! Totally, totally shocked!"

"I'm so happy for you," congratulated Josh, rushing over and giving them both big hugs.

"So very happy!" cried Bill, joining in with hugs.

"This calls for champagne," suggested Josh.

"It's right here." Lucas popped the cork and poured champagne into the glasses.

"How did this happen?" asked Bill.

Lucas handed Bill a glass. "It all started when Ami propositioned me."

Bill beamed. "I have a feeling this is going to be an extremely enjoyable story. Tell me all."

"Ami, it would be my pleasure to host a celebration dinner at the club for you and Lucas next weekend."

"Oh, Sharon, that's very thoughtful and generous, but the reason we slipped away is because we didn't want any fuss."

"I promise it will be a small and tasteful celebration. Close friends only. Of course, I would be happy to host your families as well."

"I don't know," hesitated Ami. She was currently feeling a little overwhelmed by this surprise mini bridal lunch Sharon, Meg and Elise had sprung on her.

The three of them had become her good friends since she had moved to Cypress Nest. Ami had bought what had been Elise's renovated guest house. Meg was the real estate agent who had sold it to her. And Sharon was the local wealthy widow who had helped Ami collect clues to solve a murder shortly after she'd moved in. Ami enjoyed and treasured their friendship.

"Honey, just agree," coaxed Meg.

"Ami, please," added Elise. "Marriage is a major event in life and worth celebrating. We want to toast you."

"Okay, let me check how Lucas feels about it and I'll let you know."

"Arthur approached Lucas and was informed he will abide by your decision," updated Sharon.

"Say yes," ordered Meg.

"Okay, yes, but no decorations or gifts. Just a simple dinner. Promise?"

"Promise," agreed Sharon.

"Now that that's settled, what's the deal with living arrangements? Which house are you selling? And I insist on the listing," said Meg.

"Why is it always about business with you?" accused Elise.

"Hey, I have to work for my supper."

"Lucas has decided to sell his house. And, of course, he'll give you the listing."

"Thanks, Honey. You've made the right decision. I mean about which house to sell. His house is big, pristine and right in town. I can get him top price."

"How do you know it's pristine?" asked Elise.

"One look at his landscaping. Plus, Carl and I stopped by last Christmas to drop off some cookies and I got to see the inside."

"Cookies? Really, Meg?" challenged Elise.

"Okay, I had a buyer who wanted a house in town. Lucas wasn't interested in selling, but he gave me a tour and it was as clean inside as it is outside."

"Of course, it is. He has a cleaning lady and he practically lives at work," said Ami.

"I'm glad Lucas is selling." Elise reached over and gave Ami a hug. "That way, we'll still be neighbors."

"I would have hated to move. I love my house. It has my studio and that wonderful ocean-front deck. Lucas feels as comfortable there as I do. He said he's looking forward to not having any yard work. I'm so happy it all worked out."

"Lucas isn't the only change coming to your neighborhood," hinted Meg.

"Lou's selling his house," said Elise.

"He's moving?"

"Yes," confirmed Elise, "in with me."

"That's wonderful!" congratulated Ami.

"It's about time," said Meg. "You've been dating for twenty years."

"What an exaggeration! We didn't start dating until after I left soaps. So, it's been about three years."

"Seems like twenty."

"Need I remind you Lucy was alive until six years ago?" clarified Sharon.

"I admit I was reluctant to commit to a widower. Lou and Lucy were so devoted and I was insecure about the comparisons. How do you live up to ghostly perfection? But Lou has never once compared me to Lucy. So, that helped me feel ready."

"It's obvious Lou has moved on with his life and is devoted to you now," said Ami.

"She's just not used to nice guys. Married three egotistical jerks," snarled Meg.

"To be honest, I wasn't easy to live with either."

"But you didn't cheat on them," defended Meg.

"That's true, but relationships are mine fields, especially for actors juggling insecurities and egos."

"It must be refreshing to enjoy a relationship without that type of pressure," suggested Ami.

"It's a lot less stressful. It helps that my ego isn't as needy as it used to be. Turns out, community theater and the occasional cameo satisfy it. I'm content with enjoying a more loving and peaceful life."

"Good, because you need to make this relationship work. I have a buyer and Lou's house will be sold by next week." Meg turned to Sharon. "Why don't you and Arthur jump on board? He practically lives at your place anyway. And I'd love to get my hands on that estate of his. It's worth a fortune." She rubbed her palms together.

"We prefer our relationship as is, thank you very much."

"What about moving forward in your relationship, Meg?" prodded Elise.

"I'd be willing, but Carl still has battle fatigue from that nasty divorce and hefty settlement to his ex."

"That was four years ago. I think he's commitment shy, like I was about Lou."

"I can't blame him for being cautious. Few people run off and get married after their first, to put it tactfully, union," purred Meg, staring at Ami.

"I'm not discussing something so personal."

"Then, it may dismay you to hear that Bill is discussing it all over town," advised Sharon.

"Are you serious?"

"Honey, gossip is flying about how you propositioned Lucas and so charmed him, he proposed in the morning."

"How dare Bill? This is so embarrassing."

"That's why it's so juicy," teased Elise. "So, I have to know, did you or didn't you proposition Lucas?"

"Of course, not. I simply asked him if he'd like to have sex."

"Impressive. Wouldn't have pegged you to be so forward," complimented Meg.

"Actually, that was a smart move," noted Elise. "Never hurts to test compatibility before committing."

"For the record," informed Sharon, "that request you made to Lucas would be considered a proposition."

CHAPTER FOUR

The Inquiry

"Oh, this theater is beautiful," whispered Ami. "I didn't expect it to be so luxurious or so large."

"We have seating for an audience of five hundred," explained Sharon. "And you have no need to whisper. Empty stage at the moment." She nodded to the front of the theater.

"And look how plush these seats are," appreciated Ami, rubbing the back of one. She sat down. "Soft and comfy. Most of the community plays I've attended had seats a grade above folding chairs."

"The comfortable seating allows the audience to focus solely on the performance."

"Well, this is a really grand theater," raved Ami.

"I agree. All thanks to Sharon's generosity," greeted Randall Griffin, smiling broadly as he walked up to them.

Sharon Hart Randall, philanthropist and major contributor to the Cypress Nest Community Theater, was happily accommodated by cast and crew whenever she dropped by.

"Hello, Randall, I believe you know Ami."

"Yes. Nice to see you again. Heard about you and Lucas. Congratulations."

"Thanks. I'm so impressed with your theater. It must be a pleasure working here."

"It is. Grateful for such top notch equipment. We boast a full lighting grid and sound system. They're computer-controlled from a booth at the back of the auditorium and from a soundboard by the orchestra pit. Come on, I'll show you."

Randall led them to the front of the theater.

Ami looked down into the pit. "It's deeper and larger than I'd expect."

"Space for twenty musicians and their instruments, but most productions use less than a dozen."

"And that stage is huge," admired Ami.

"It's fifty feet wide and twenty feet tall."

"Oh, look! My portrait of Elise is part of the set design."

"Yes, Bill suggested it," said Randall. "The scene represents her character's living room and party."

"The set is another splendid contribution by Bill," noted Sharon.

"Give him a script and he hits it out of the park. Don't know how we'd manage without him."

Sharon turned with a question toward Randall. "Is that Josh's piano on stage?"

"Yes. The scene's a current day Porter-esque type party. Bill thought it'd be a natural fit."

"I am impressed he managed agreement from Josh."

Randall chuckled. "David and I had to swear an oath not to give him any lines."

"I don't understand," said Ami. "Josh is often on stage. He's an experienced performer."

"As a pianist, yes. You won't get him to sing or recite lines. Which leads me to a request, more of a beg, really. We badly need extras to beef up the party scene. No lines. Just quietly sitting on sofas and chairs on stage. Could I interest the two of you in helping us out?" he asked, adding quickly, "Promise it won't be time consuming. No rehearsals until dress. And no wardrobe fittings. Wear your own party clothes, neutral colors so you'll blend into the set."

"I would be happy to accommodate. How about you, Ami?"

"It sounds like fun. You can count on me, too."

"Wonderful! Let me give the good news to David. He'll be thrilled," replied Randall, hurrying away.

"Since we have agreed to be extras, shall we continue our tour to the stage?" suggested Sharon.

Ami followed Sharon up the steps. They wandered around the stage, looking closely at the props and, finally, settled beside one another on one of the sofas.

"Do you imagine yourself comfortable on stage, Ami?"

"I expect I'll be nervous when there's an audience staring at us. But I still want to do it. You seem relaxed. I gather you've done this before?"

"A number of times. They often need a last minute extra. On one occasion, I was given a line."

"What was the line? Do you remember?"

"Of course. 'He went that way,'" she voiced, extending her arm. Smiling, she summarized, "Clearly, the focal point of the play."

"I can tell you enjoy this. Your eyes brightened when Randall asked us to be extras and, again now, when you repeated the line. Why aren't you part of the cast?"

"We found, very early on, that our musicals pull in the biggest audience. Singing is not my forte."

"Surely there are non-singing parts."

"Not interested. Cast members invest a significant amount of time. As an extra, I can experience the pleasure without the pain."

Ami lowered her voice and leaned toward Sharon. "Do you think the singers are here yet? I'd love a chance to speak with Kathy Riggs."

"I am sure that can be arranged," whispered Sharon. She raised her voice slightly. "Shall we resume our tour backstage?"

Ami followed Sharon backstage. They approached the nearest group standing together chatting.

"Excuse me for interrupting," greeted Sharon, "but I wanted to make a point of thanking you for donating your time, talent and hard work. I know you will make this year's fundraiser a success. I think many of you know Ami."

Several in the group murmured they did.

"This theater is very impressive. When Sharon said backstage, I expected a dim hallway. This is a bright and roomy area!"

"The total space measures eighty feet wide, forty feet tall and thirty feet deep," explained Sharon. "It is divided for three uses. To the right are several dressing rooms with showers."

"You mean like for the stars of the show?"

"Mainly, but they're shared with all of us when needed," said Cindy Wilson. "It's nice to see you again, Ami."

"You, too, Cindy." Ami knew her as a real estate associate of Meg. "So, tell me about the part you're playing?"

"I'm not on stage. I'm in the pit. I play violin in the orchestra."

"I had no idea you played violin. You must be very talented to be in the orchestra."

"A few of us local musicians join the student orchestra for productions each year. I'm considered more a contributing violinist than a talent."

"Well, I consider you a talent. Congratulations."

"I understand congratulations are in order for you, too. Meg told me about you and Lucas getting married. Much happiness."

"Thanks. I'm in awe of your beautiful theater. It's so impressive. What's behind those large, double doors over there?"

"Storage area for costumes, sets and props," informed Cindy.

"It is equipped with an electronic outer door to provide drive-up capability," continued Sharon. "This wall adjoining the stage is two massive panels that provide access for moving furniture and equipment.

"The great part is it's sound-proofed," contributed Will Lawson, one of the actors. He was also the brother of Malcolm Lawson, the male lead of the musical. Ami had been introduced to both of them at the club. She'd even danced with Will a few times. "Allows us freedom to get rowdy back here. This is considered our green room."

"It's very well equipped." Ami noticed a complete kitchen with a French-door refrigerator. Along the wall were two white-clothed buffet tables. The first had two large urns, labeled coffee and hot water, with containers of tea bags, sugar and cream next to them. The rest of the table was filled with a line of thermos bottles. The second table held pitchers of iced water and glasses, and trays of fruits, crudités, cookies and candy.

"I can't get over how big this theater is. Even your cast is larger than I expected. I had no idea how many of you were contributing your talents," complimented Ami.

"Mostly everyone in this community eventually ends up involved with the theater in some way," said Cindy. "It's the center of everything."

"Fortunately, we have a wealth of talent in our community," stated David Carson, the stage director, coming up behind them.

"And we are fortunate to have you, David, expertly leading us," replied Sharon.

"Well, it's been difficult the past week. Losing Justin was a blow to us all, but we're pulling together and soldiering through. I understand you'll both be joining our cast as extras. I'm delighted. Thank you for helping out."

Ami noticed one of the female cast move quickly out the side door. A moment later, a male followed her.

"We are looking forward to it, David," replied Sharon. She turned to Ami. "Shall we be on our way?"

Ami nodded.

Once they were out of ear-range of the group, Sharon whispered, "Kathy Riggs is the one who left the room."

"Oh, good, let's catch her outside."

They found Kathy sitting on a bench, wiping tears from her eyes. The male who had followed her had his arm around her.

"Hello, Kathy, Roger. May I help?" asked Sharon, walking up to them.

"David mentioning Justin overwhelmed me," said Kathy.

"That's certainly understandable," sympathized Sharon, sitting down beside her.

"I suppose you heard he was poisoned," said Kathy.

"Yes. I am sorry."

Roger stood. "Now that you have additional support, do you mind my going back, Kathy? Break's almost over."

"Go ahead. I'll be there in a few minutes. Thanks, Roger."

He nodded to Sharon and Ami before turning and walking into the building.

Watching Roger leave, Kathy murmured, "Can't believe how supportive he's been after..." She stopped speaking.

"After?" nudged Ami.

"Roger and I were fairly serious once. My friendship with Justin caused our break up. I know he felt hurt, but he never made a big deal about it. He started dating Sally. They seem happy together and I'm happy for them."

"It seems like he understood and moved on. We can't help who we fall in love with," ventured Ami.

"Yes, I was in love with Justin. We seriously cared for one another, but we weren't having an affair, I swear. Justin did not cheat on Shelby," emphasized Kathy. "We were close friends. He confided in me."

"Since you were close friends, do you have any idea who might have done this to him?"

"It was Shelby, of course."

"Really? You have evidence?"

"Nothing tangible. But Justin was planning to divorce her. That's why she killed him."

"But I don't understand. Rumor has it she wanted to see other men. If Justin divorced her, she'd be free. So she'd have no reason to kill him," surmised Ami.

"She wanted freedom, but the divorce was going to trigger their prenup. It would have cost her a bundle."

"Had Justin told her he was filing for divorce?"

"Yes, the weekend before he died. That's why I know it was her who did it. It would have been easy for her. She always readied his thermos."

"So, you think the potassium was in his thermos?"

"I know it was. That's how I got sick. I drank some of his herbal coffee by mistake. And further proof is that his thermos was missing afterward."

"How do you know it went missing?"

"I had stayed behind because I wasn't feeling well. I went backstage to get some of my tea and noticed the empty space next to mine. That's where Justin's thermos had been."

"But Shelby was at the hospital with Justin. She couldn't have removed the thermos."

"She could have asked one of her boyfriends to do it for her."

"Wouldn't he have suspected something?"

"Why would he? Everyone thought Justin had a heart attack. What's suspicious about her asking someone to bring home Justin's thermos to save her a trip."

“Have you informed the police of all this?”

“Yes. Lucas questioned me at the hospital.”

“Lucas is fortunate you’re such an observant and cooperative witness. I’m sure the information you provided will be very helpful to him.”

“Thanks. I heard about the two of you getting married. Congratulations.”

“Thank you. Since you’re at rehearsal today, I assume you’re feeling better.”

“Physically, I’m fine. Emotionally, my heart breaks that Justin wasn’t as lucky as me.” She stared intently at Ami before continuing. “I heard you helped Lucas last year with those murders. Can you help him get the evidence that proves Shelby’s guilt? We can’t let her get away with this.”

Ami hesitated for a moment, not sure exactly how she should respond.

“If Ami is willing to make inquiries, I will finance it,” quickly announced Sharon.

“Thank you.” Kathy reached out and squeezed Sharon’s hand in appreciation. “I’ve got to get back.” She offered them a weak smile and ran back into the theater.

Ami turned to Sharon. “Just what do you plan on financing?”

“You could hardly promise to interfere with your husband’s investigation. My offer was an obvious gesture to rescue you with an ulterior motive of keeping the lines of communication open with Kathy. I would assume her close relationship with Justin is beneficial to you.”

“Thanks, and good thinking,” applauded Ami. “Our next step is to verify as much of this as possible with Bill.”

>=<

“Yes, Kathy is correct. Justin planned to divorce Shelby. His attorney had everything ready.”

"Why didn't you mention the divorce before?"

"I promised Justin not to speak of it to anyone. Surely, Ami, you realize how difficult that was for me, but I was honoring my promise. I kept my word, until now."

"Justin would be proud of you for maintaining his confidence."

"Thank you, chère Sharon."

"Bill what can you tell us about that prenup of theirs?" asked Ami.

"I only know that prior to their marriage, he had his attorney draw up a prenup. He never confided the details, assuming I'd gossip about them, which I would have."

"Sharon, do you think you can make some calls and see if you can find out what's in it?"

"Of course."

"Thanks. Bill, Kathy seemed sure the prenup was the reason Shelby killed Justin. I know you said you didn't think Shelby would do it, but isn't it possible?"

"Anything is possible. But Shelby isn't nearly as diabolical as Kathy believes. She dislikes Shelby because she was in love with Justin herself."

"Kathy swears they weren't having an affair. Do you believe that?"

"Yes. They had a close emotional bond, but it wasn't physical."

"Shelby was having affairs. Wouldn't Justin have reasoned if she was, why shouldn't he?"

"No. I'm certain he would not. Justin was a man of integrity."

Ami realized questioning Justin's character was causing Bill to become defensive. She decided to change the subject. "Is Kathy married?"

"Divorced," said Bill.

"Did she inherit or does she work?"

"She has a medical insurance billing business that she operates out of her home. Most of the local doctors use her."

"She said she dated Roger Swanson but spent so much time with Justin, they broke up. True?"

"Yes. Roger really cared for her and was hurt by her relationship with Justin."

"That gives him a motive. Do you think he'll get back together with Kathy now that Justin's gone? He made a point of comforting her at the theater."

"That was probably because he and Kathy still consider one another friends. He's moved on to the very attractive Sally Kirby. Rumor has it they're a devoted couple. I don't see a reason for him to go back in time."

"I assume Kathy was looking forward to Justin's divorce?"

"Perhaps envisioning herself as the next Mrs. Gibson?" interjected Sharon.

"Well, there's truth in that," agreed Bill. "I think Justin would have married Kathy. He trusted her. He could relax and be himself with her. And they shared singing and gardening interests. They were well-matched."

"Are you implying he and Shelby were not well-matched?"

"They were not."

"So, why did he marry her?"

Bill sighed. "I think passion and ego. Justin found Shelby exciting. She's young and attractive. He was flattered by her interest in him. It was a whirlwind romance. They married within a few months of meeting. I think if they'd had a longer courtship, their differences would have become evident and the marriage never would have taken place."

"That's his reason. What was hers? Why'd she marry him?"

"I don't know for sure, but I've always had the impression Shelby was searching for something. My guess is she thought she'd found it with Justin and then realized that she hadn't."

"Is it possible that Justin would have changed his mind about divorcing Shelby?"

"No. Justin couldn't trust her. She'd made a fool of him. He felt embarrassed."

"So he needed to save face by divorcing her," rephrased Ami.

"It was much more than that. Her affairs were the final tipping point. Justin had seriously thought about this divorce for some time. It wasn't a whim. Within months of their marriage, he realized she'd lost interest in him. And he found her self-centeredness more and more irritating. Neither was happy in the relationship. He wanted it over. And once Justin made up his mind about something, he followed through."

"Both you and Roselyn said Justin's children didn't like Shelby. Roselyn gave me her reason. Why do you think they didn't like her?" asked Ami.

"Shelby was fifteen years younger than Justin. His children assumed she was a gold digger who married their father for his money. Not true, of course."

"According to what Roselyn said and Sharon confirmed, Shelby was better off than Justin. Did he tell his kids that?"

"Yes, but it made no difference. They continued to dislike her and refused to accept her. Their distancing themselves distressed him. But, as you know, children can misunderstand, form wrong impressions and lash out in hurtful ways." He tilted his head and raised his eyebrows.

"Yes, I do know. I assume you're probing for an update about my daughter and sister. Correct?"

"Correct. Are you going to comply?"

Ami shook her finger at him. "You're incorrigible. It's a good thing I love you."

"I love you, too. Now, out with it."

"As it currently stands, their shock over my marriage has turned to anger and neither is speaking to me."

"Now, I understand why neither has replied to my dinner invitation," murmured Sharon.

"I'm sorry they didn't have the courtesy to reply."

"Unimportant," dismissed Sharon. "I am sorry they have chosen such a painful stance."

"I'm just thankful Teddy still texts me. I sent him a brief text that I'd remarried. He must have heard his mother and father discussing it because he replied that both he and his dad are happy for me and that he loves me very much."

"There, you see, mon cher ami, not all your daughter's family has forsaken you."

"Hopefully, Shirley won't put a stop to our texts."

"I doubt she'd do that. Teddy's not a child."

"He's fourteen, Bill. That's still a child and, yes, she could put a stop to it."

"What are you going to do about her?"

"Nothing. Like you said, children lash out. I have no control over her feelings and actions. My love for her hasn't changed, but neither has my love for Lucas. I've chosen a life with him. If she wants to be angry over my marriage, that's her choice."

"Although we are not family, your friends love you and we will be there for you," promised Sharon.

"Yes, you can count on us. Josh and I may not be blood, but we consider you a member of our family." He leaned over and kissed Ami's cheek.

"Thank you. I'm grateful to have such caring friends."

>=<

Ami and Sharon relaxed over lunch, discussing Ami's latest portrait commission and Sharon's latest charity project.

Sharon returned to the subject of Justin's death by pulling out her phone. "I suppose we should resume. According to my notes, Shelby is our main suspect."

"Our only suspect at the moment. Bill had doubts about her guilt and he's a good judge of people. Plus, he and Justin were very close so he had an inside view that others didn't."

"I sense the addition of a but."

"The but is Shelby had the motive and the opportunity. We need to discover who else had a reason for wanting Justin dead. Motives are mainly about money or love."

"As for love, there is Kathy," reminded Sharon.

"Yes, but Bill said Justin was set on divorce which means Kathy's window of opportunity was opening, not closing. She'd have no reason to kill him. I think we've been looking at this from the wrong direction."

"What do you mean?"

"Everyone's focus has been around Shelby, the obvious suspect. I think we should be focusing on Justin, the victim. The more we know about him, the better chance of discovering who else might have a motive for killing him," explained Ami.

"You mean what was behind his façade? Perhaps a secret life he was hiding? That sort of inquiry?"

"Exactly. Maybe he was a secret gambler and indebted to someone, or maybe he was involved in a ruthless business dealing."

"Bill never mentioned any transgressions of that nature and he was quite open about the rest."

"Bill told us what he *knew*," emphasized Ami, "but what about all he didn't know. He admitted Justin withheld information from him because of gossiping."

"Still, I doubt Justin had secrets of that kind. Bill was his confidant. His closest friend for over many years. Surely, he would have been aware at some point."

"Marianne and I are close, but I kept marrying Lucas a secret until it was a done deal, even though I knew she would be thrilled for us. She would have blabbed, and it was important my daughter heard it directly from me."

"Alright, then," conceded Sharon, making entries into her phone as she spoke, "in addition to inquiring about the prenup, I will probe for investments, losses, debts, etc."

"Wonderful! The fuller the financial picture, the better."

>=<

"So, how is your investigation coming along?" asked Lucas over dinner.

Ami looked up, innocently. "What do you mean?"

"Perhaps a few details will sharpen your memory. You and Sharon interviewed Kathy Riggs at the theater. By the way, congratulations on joining the cast. Then, the two of you had a tête-à-tête with Bill, followed by lunch at the club. I assume to sort through your findings and design a plan of action. After which, Sharon made a number of phone calls to attorneys and accountants."

Ami's mouth dropped open.

"Oh, I see it's coming back to you."

"If you had me followed, I'll be very upset with you."

"First of all, I'm insulted you'd think I'd do that. Secondly, no need to have you followed. People walk up to me and volunteer your comings and goings as a matter of conversation."

"What's that suppose to mean?"

"You don't seem to realize what a celebrity you've become. Fellow community members are still fascinated with your involvement in last year's murders. And, now, with this current murder, not to mention Bill's gossip about the brazen way you got me to marry you, they are watching your every move with delight."

"Surely you're joking."

"I wish I were. I don't enjoy having my day interrupted with updates on my wife's activities. I have plenty to keep me busy."

Amy reached over and touched his arm. "I'm sorry gossip about me pulled your focus. I know how stressful and dangerous your work is."

He patted her hand. "Don't worry about it, Columbo."

"You realize only people our age know that character reference. You don't use it at work, do you?"

"Current characters probably would be more relatable. How about Verlaque?"

"I doubt any of your young police officers watch BritBox."

"Well, our friends do. You said you were hoping for a second season. I thought you enjoyed that show?"

"Lucas, focus. Don't you find someone spying on me creepy? Who reported all this to you?"

"I'll tell you if you promise not to confront them."

"Them? More than one person talked about me?"

"Yes."

"Well, who are they?"

"First, promise me."

"I promise."

"What are you promising to?"

"You're getting pretty nitpicky about this."

"Can you blame me?"

Ami grinned mischievously. "No."

"Didn't expect you to admit it. Well?"

"Okay, I promise not to confront the people who talked about me."

"Thank you. Randall mentioned you being at the theater. Josh mentioned your meeting with Bill. Meg saw you and Sharon at the club."

"Why didn't she come over?"

"She was with a client."

"And, obviously, it was Arthur who called you about Sharon's phone calls," finished Ami. "He's convinced I'm going to get her killed."

"He's not entirely wrong about the danger and you know that," cautioned Lucas.

"That's why, after dinner, I had planned to report every single thing we discovered today."

He raised an eyebrow.

"Well, more like an overview," amended Ami.

"Then, don't hold me in suspense. What did you discover?"

>=<

"The details of the prenup clearly explain why Shelby did not want a divorce," revealed Sharon.

"Wonderful! Run it down for me," urged Ami.

"The financial part of their prenup agreement is fairly standard. Shelby's inheritance was deemed non-marital property, as was Justin's trust to his children. Their infidelity clause is the interesting part. It granted Justin one million dollars if Shelby was caught cheating on him, but there was no reciprocal clause."

"So Shelby had to pay Justin for cheating on him, but Justin didn't have to pay Shelby if he cheated on her?" clarified Ami.

"Correct. That typically happens when one partner has a documented history of infidelity."

"So we can conclude that Justin was aware of Shelby's past."

"Yes. And there was another clause stating if the marriage ended in divorce in less than two years' time due to infidelity on Shelby's part, Justin would be entitled to another one million in addition to the typical asset division from the marital property. Justin's lawyer did an excellent job on that prenup."

"Were they married less than two years?" asked Ami.

"One year, three months, twenty-four days. And the pièce de résistance is Justin's attorney had divorce papers ready to serve."

"Between the infidelity and marriage agreements, Shelby would have had to pay Justin a total of two million dollars and the divorce was closing in on her. That's a hefty motive," judged Ami.

"Agreed."

"Seems our focus has returned to Shelby."

CHAPTER FIVE

The Celebration

Ami smiled broadly. "Mom, Marianne, it's so wonderful to see you. Thank you so much for coming." She looked beyond them, hopefully.

"Sorry, Darling," whispered Ami's mother, Claire, leaning in to kiss her cheek. "It's just us."

"I didn't really expect them to come," admitted Ami.

"No harm in hoping. Maybe someday, huh?" She offered her an encouraging smile.

Ami smiled back.

Marianne ran up and gave her a hug. "Aunt Ami, I'm so happy for you. I've been hoping all along you two would get together, but you really surprised us by getting married. Mike said to tell you he loves you and he's sorry he couldn't fly out. He's in the middle of finalizing everything at work for the move."

"Tell him I love him, too, and I understand. We'll have plenty of time to visit once you're settled in your new home."

Marianne let go of her aunt and moved on to Lucas. "Welcome to the family, Uncle Lucas," she said, giving him a big hug.

Lucas stared at her with a startled expression.

"What? You don't want me to call you uncle?"

"I like it. I'm just surprised how naturally it flowed from you."

"I think I've been subconsciously practicing it since I met you."

"It's nice to know you were supporting me. By the way," he leaned in and lowered his voice, "congratulations. Ami told me about the baby, but I understand you're not announcing it yet."

"We finally told our parents so I guess it's not a secret anymore. Well, not to anyone who knows my mother," she laughed.

"Welcome," greeted Sharon, joining them. "You must be Claire Martin, Ami's mother. It is a pleasure to meet you," she extended her hand.

Claire grasped it. "Thanks for inviting us. It's nice to meet you, too. "

"Marianne, very nice to see you again. Come. Allow me to introduce you to everyone. I especially would like you to meet Lucas' parents. Marianne, I believe you know most of the other guests," Sharon added, as they walked toward the private dining room she had reserved.

Ami was grateful Sharon was performing the hostess duties this evening. She needed a moment to regroup. Her daughter and sister not coming tonight disappointed her more than she had expected.

Lucas touched her shoulder. "If you need a few minutes away from here, I'll be happy to walk outside with you."

"I knew they wouldn't come, but that secret little part of me that was hoping feels shattered."

He wrapped his arms tightly around her. "I know it hurts. Your family is important to you. I'm sorry our marriage is causing you pain. Are you feeling regrets?"

"I promise you I have no regrets. I truly love being married to you."

"And I'm the happiest I've ever been. Even my most gruesome work days are easier knowing I'm coming home to you."

She smiled up at him. "At this very moment, I have an overwhelming urge to celebrate our marriage. Let's go join the others."

>=<

Audrey Duncan was strolling the Cypress Cottage Bed and Breakfast garden when she came upon Claire Martin sitting in a corner by a waterfall. "Oh, Claire, sorry to disturb you. I didn't expect anyone else to be up this early."

"I've always been an early riser. You're welcome to join me, unless you'd prefer to wonder in solitude."

"Isn't this garden an enchanting oasis?" gushed Audrey, taking a seat beside Claire.

"Enchanting is the perfect description. It has a magical quality."

"I heard it was featured in *Gardening Today*. I can understand why. I'd love to have a garden this lush and nurturing to roam every day."

"It's not only the garden, this whole bed and breakfast experience has been nurturing. It was generous of Bill and Josh to host us this weekend."

"Yes, it was. I've thoroughly enjoyed this weekend. One never knows when visiting for the first time what the tone will be," Audrey confided, "but everyone has made a point of being warm and welcoming."

"Yes, they have."

"I'm delighted Lucas and Ami found one another. Lucas mentioned Ami a number of times over the past year. He told me he fell in love with her the first time they danced. I'm a hopeless romantic so I was cheering for them."

"Personality wise, they seem a solid match, too. That's important," noted Claire.

"I agree and I'm relieved," admitted Audrey.

"Relieved?"

"Yes. Lucas and his ex had little in common. After they moved here, she spent most of her time back in LA. They had different interests and were living separate lives. I considered their divorce a blessing for both of them."

"They just weren't suited," concluded Claire.

"Seeing Lucas so happy with Ami gives me a sense of peace."

"I understand what you mean. I feel a sense of peace about Ami, too. She was hiding in her memories of her late husband. I'm relieved she decided to allow herself to love again."

"It seems no matter how old they get, we mothers never cease to worry."

"So true."

>=<

"Bill and Josh have been helping me with the interior design and purchases for our new house. I would have been lost without them," bubbled Marianne.

The families had gathered in the garden for a farewell lunch celebration before heading home.

"I'd love to hear your plans," encouraged Audrey.

"Bill's the one who came up with the plan. He's amazing. Go ahead. Tell them," ordered Marianne.

"It is a flexible plan because Marianne is an explosion of creative ideas."

"Bill had to reign me in."

"I try, but she doesn't tame easily. Honestly, it's been a pleasure working on their home. The bones of the home are a designer's dream and they weren't exaggerating when they said move in ready. The floors are exquisitely fitted claro walnut in perfect shape. And, best of all, the walls were a perfect canvas of white which saved us the lengthy nightmare of removing wallpaper or sealing over brash colors. The rooms are large and open, and the massive windows fill the rooms with light."

"You'd love the location, Audrey," assured Claire. "It's high on a hill with a marvelous ocean view."

"Sounds wonderful! I expect you'll be accentuated that view, Bill."

"Yes. We're installing motorized window blinds that can be totally hidden or configured for the sunrise and set. To keep the focus on the view, we're using neutrals for the basic furniture pieces."

"We're going to pop the rooms with colorful accents like we did for your home, Aunt Ami," interjected Marianne.

"You did it beautifully in my home, Dear. I'm sure it will be even more impressive in a large home like yours."

"And I love what Bill came up with for the nursery! We've used several shades of soft yellows and the wall by the crib will be stenciled with lots and lots of colorful balloons with positive phrases in them. It will create a feeling that's uplifting and floating with loving energy."

"That sounds like a happy environment for a new baby," agreed Audrey.

"Ooh, I forgot to tell you about my most important purchase, my baby grand piano! Josh picked it out. It's a lot larger than I would have chosen, but he said I had to have a six-footer because of the sound. Tell them why, Josh," urged Marianne.

"There's an enhanced tonal quality with the larger size. Marianne kept insisting I choose one for her, but I found that difficult. The touch, tone, sound, echo are all subjective. I'm partial to the Fazioli F156, but a Steinway seemed better suited for Marianne's deliberate touch."

"He's nicely saying I pound on it. I wouldn't have had a clue what to buy without Josh. He knew about plates and soundboards and strings. I had no idea those things were important. I just wanted an ebony one."

"Dad's had a Steinway for years," offered Lucas. "He plays all the time."

"I'm not a professional, like Josh, but I've been playing since I was a child and can manage a number of classics without making my wife run out of the room," he chuckled.

"He's being modest. Daniel is an excellent pianist," complimented Audrey. "He plays almost daily and fills our home with enjoyable music."

"I plan to fill our home with music, too. Hopefully, I'll learn to make it enjoyable. I took lessons as a child, but haven't played in years. Josh found a teacher in Monterey to help me get back into it."

"It seems you have everything under control and are moving smoothly along," remarked Audrey.

"Thanks to Bill. He rescued me. I jumped right in without realizing how big a project this was. Suddenly, I was in over my head and starting to panic. Bill coordinated everything with a timetable. He's a genius."

"It's been mon plaisir working with you again, mon très cher."

"Bill, je ne savais pas que tu parlais français. C'est une langue tellement romantique," said Audrey.

"I agree the language is romantic, but I'm not fluent, one semester of French at Berkley. I love the sound of a phrase here and there and confess I use it for affect."

"Granny's fluent in about ten languages. She used to travel all over the world as a photographer."

"That sounds an exciting career," said Audrey. "It must be wonderful to speak so many languages."

"Marianne exaggerates. I had to learn phrases in a number of languages to accommodate my needs, but I speak fluently in only four, French being my favorite."

"I'm proof of that. Her love of French caused her to spell Ami with an 'i' instead of a 'y.' My name's been mispronounced all my life."

"I never meant it to be a burden. I thought it was clever. Simply didn't think about the problems it would cause. I apologize, Darling."

"Well, Mom, as the French would say, 'ce qui est fait est fait.' So, Marianne, tell us when you'll be moving into your new home?"

"Soon. All the big projects are completed. The furniture arrived last week and Bill's coming next week for the fun part, all the accessories. By the time Mike gets here, everything should be finished."

"I'm sure Mike appreciates all your hard work."

"He does, Aunt Ami, but, truth is, other than his home office, he could care less about the décor."

"It's because he knows Marianne will steamroll all the decisions anyway," added Bill.

"He's right. Once I get excited about something there's no stopping me. I can't help it."

"I have to say I envy your considerable energy and enthusiasm," complimented Audrey. "Bill, did you find it hard keeping up?"

"The first project we collaborated on was Ami's home. I learned the hard way that Marianne's normal speed is fast forward. This time, the distance between us meant most of our interactions were on-line which offered me personal rest periods."

>=<

"That was the most uncomfortable celebration of life, I've ever attended," grumbled Elise, as she, Meg and Ami stepped into Sharon's limousine.

"It was quite distressing," agreed Sharon. "The unspoken anger toward Shelby was palpable."

"Well, Shelby deserved it given that stunt she pulled with Ethan. What was she thinking?"

"I don't know, Meg. I guess he was supposed to be part of her support system, but he was a poor choice," said Elise.

"She had Roselyn for support. Having Ethan sit beside her was outright disrespect," snarled Meg.

"I agree, it was a questionable choice," deemed Sharon.

"Maybe it was a deliberate choice," suggested Ami.

"What do you mean?" asked Elise.

"I think she had Ethan sit beside her to send a message."

"Was the message, 'I was unfaithful to my husband. Here's one of the men I cheated with?'"

"Meg, really!" chided Elise, before giggling.

"It's true," maintained Meg.

"She was declaring her innocence."

"What innocence? Honey, everyone knows she cheated."

"Not innocence of cheating, Meg, innocence of killing Justin," clarified Ami.

"I believe I understand your point," said Sharon. "Ethan's presence was meant to convey she had nothing to hide; ergo, she must be innocent of killing her husband."

"If that was her message; ergo, no one bought it," fired Meg.

"Justin's kids sure didn't," added Elise. "They shot her some hateful looks."

"Surprised one of them didn't pull out a gun."

"Quite an exaggeration, Meg," asserted Sharon.

"Honey, it happens. And it didn't help she never shed a tear."

"Grief is personal. Some people aren't comfortable crying in public," defended Ami.

"Maybe not, but you'd think she'd show some signs of grief, like smudged mascara or dark circles. She was bright-eyed, makeup perfect. Kathy Riggs, on the other hand, looked more like the grieving widow. Her grief was raw. I admit I felt sorry for her."

"Oh, me, too," admitted Elise. "I almost broke down watching her."

"There's no doubt she and Justin had a lot more than friendship going on."

"Both Kathy and Bill said it was only platonic," interjected Ami.

"Well, Bill's rarely wrong. If he said it wasn't physical, it's probably true," yielded Meg. "In any case, you could tell she really cared about him."

"It was heart wrenching," said Elise. "I was pleased to see Roger and Sally supporting her."

"I think Sally thought Roger was a little too supportive. She shot him a couple of ticked-off looks."

"Don't make something out of nothing, Meg," cautioned Elise. "Both were being supportive of Kathy."

"You know, Meg brought up something I'm curious about," noted Ami. "Bill said Roger and Kathy remained friends after their breakup. He comforted her at the theater and then again today. I noticed Sally bristle once, too. Do you think Roger wants to get back together with Kathy?"

"No," said Elise. "Roger and Sally are in love."

"You're such a pushover when it comes to love," accused Meg. "He's been pining for Kathy all along, using Sally as a fill in. Mark my words, he's going to dump her."

"Not true," disputed Elise. "Sally's my understudy so we talk all the time. They're really in love."

"Your understudy? I thought she was in the chorus."

"Both. Most of the ensemble have to understudy other roles, Ami."

"Did Justin understudy a leading role?"

"Yes. Malcolm's."

"Who is doing it now?"

"Malcolm's brother, Will."

Ami tucked that information away for future investigation.

"I can see how Roger would be attracted to Sally," mused Meg. "She has sex appeal. Men are so visual. They pant over boobs and butts and flowing hair, ignoring most of it's fake."

"Sally's hair is real, no extensions. It makes me a little jealous," admitted Elise.

"Honey, forget about her hair, her major attraction is acting out those books she writes."

"Sally is a writer?"

"Ami, surely you've heard of Sally Kirby?" Elise sounded shocked.

Ami nodded her head negatively.

"She's a bestselling romance novelist."

"Soft porn. Let's call it what it is," ripped Meg.

"I wouldn't call it that, but I agree they're very steamy. Except the point of her stories is always love. You know, how love triumphs over all and how true love is blind. I definitely believe that."

"Says the woman with a standing Botox appointment."

"I'm an actress. I have a duty to my fans to maintain my looks. I won't apologize for that. Anyway, I stand firm that Sally and Roger are in love and it warmed my heart to see them both being supportive of Kathy."

"I was impressed with how supportive your entire theater group was. They all came to honor Justin today, and many stopped to comfort Kathy. It's wonderful that you're so close," praised Ami.

"We're supportive as a theater company, but we're not close. We don't socialize, other than the cast parties on opening and closing nights, and everyone's keyed up and theater focused then. It would be nice for us to have a fun evening together where we could relax and get to know one another better."

"I shall provide that. After dress rehearsal, I shall host a casual party at the club where you can mingle and socialize."

"But, Sharon, you usually host the opening night party at the theater and the closing night party at the club."

"I shall host those as well."

"That's awfully generous of you."

"Hush, Elise, let her do it," ordered Meg. "And you have to invite me and Carl. It's the perfect excuse to get him out of the house. He's become such an old stick in the mud lately. I'd love a party."

"It would be my pleasure to invite you. I am assuming, Elise, that 'cast only' would not apply to this event?"

"The traditional 'cast only' applies mainly to opening night."

"Okay, then, no reason Carl and I can't attend!"

>=<

Lucas refilled Josh's wine glass. When he went to refill Bill's, he found it full. "Bill, would you prefer something else?"

"No. This is fine. I simply forgot to drink."

"I noticed you were unusually quiet tonight. I guessed Justin's event today brought up sadness," said Ami.

"I wish it were only sadness I was feeling. I'm overwhelmed with anger!" bellowed Bill.

"Bill, please," guided Josh, placing his hand on Bill's arm.

"I'm sorry, but today's event more than failed as a celebration of Justin's wonderful life. It was outright offensive. Shelby's behavior was unbelievably insulting. Justin's children were angry and embarrassed. Justin deserved so much better."

"I can understand your being upset. I'm sorry it wasn't more what you wanted."

"Thank you, mon cher ami." Bill took a sip of wine and relaxed his shoulders.

"There were some positives," offered Josh. "There were the kind words and sweet memories shared by Justin's friends. Your words, Bill, were particularly inspiring."

"I agree. The anecdotes you shared were heartfelt and loving," added Ami.

"I was happy to do it. Still, Justin deserved to be properly celebrated. Today's event was an embarrassment to him and his children."

Josh turned to Ami and Lucas. "We did manage to soothe Justin's children before they left for home. Bill recalled happy memories of them as kids and growing up. They left feeling better."

"That was considerate of you both," said Ami.

Bill set his glass on the table and stood up and over Lucas. "I want to know what's going on with Justin's investigation. Do you have enough evidence to arrest someone?"

"I'm sorry, Bill. I won't discuss my investigation. But I have no objection to you asking Ami about hers."

"Why separate investigations? I assumed you were collaborating. Are you two at odds?" he asked, sitting back down.

"Of course not, Bill," soothed Ami. "I happily share all I find with Lucas. I understand that he can't share back. We're fine."

"I'm relieved. It would distress me to see a couple d'amoureux torn apart by Justin's la tragédie."

"No chance of that, Bill," assured Lucas. "It's all good."

"In that case, what have you found out, Ami?"

"So far, the few bits of information I've collected point to Shelby as having the greatest motive and opportunity."

"I see. I know I told you that I didn't believe she could do something like that, but her behavior today was so disrespectful, I've changed my mind."

"I think she was attempting to make a defiant statement of her innocence," suggested Ami. "It obviously didn't come off as she intended."

"If she's innocent, why feel the need to make a statement about it?" asked Josh.

"Because she knows everyone suspects her."

"Either way, it didn't work. If she's innocent, she bungled attempts to convince anyone. And if she's not, she didn't change anyone's mind about it," surmised Josh.

"Ami, Lucas, I beg you to join forces and arrest someone as soon as possible. Justin deserves to rest in peace. I need peace, too," stated Bill.

>=<

"Hi, Roselyn, it's Ami."

"Hi, Ami. Is my portrait ready?"

"Soon, needs a bit more drying. I called because I have a question about Shelby that's puzzling me. Since you're good friends, I thought maybe you'd know the answer."

"You want to know why Shelby invited Ethan to sit beside her at the celebration of life for Justin. Very poor judgment on her part."

"I agree. So, why did she do it?"

"She said she wanted him there for protection."

"Protection from whom?"

"Everyone. She's aware most people think she poisoned Justin and she's afraid."

"Has she reason to be afraid?   Has someone threatened her?" asked Ami with concern.

"No. Nothing like that. She's afraid someone will confront her with a nasty remark. I think she felt Ethan's presence would make people uncomfortable and reluctant to approach her. It worked. Very few people even offered their condolences."

"I noticed that."

"And I noticed that you and your friends were among the few who did approach her. Thanks for that."

"You're welcome.   She's lucky to have you supporting her right now. She can use a friend."

"I suppose being her friend means standing by her even when I want to shake some sense into her. Unfortunately, she isn't listening to my advice."

"What advice is that?"

"Shelby wants to move on like nothing's happened. I tried to explain to her that it's not wise for a widow to act like she's unaffected by her husband's death, especially when he's been murdered."

"I'm sorry she's not allowing herself to grieve. It's not healthy for her, and people are getting the wrong impression."

"I know. And she infuriated Justin's children."

"She obviously upset them with Ethan."

"She upset them prior to that. They offered a few suggestions for Justin's celebration of life. Shelby told them it was all arranged, but it wasn't. Ami, she hadn't planned anything at all for Justin. Well, after they asked, she felt obliged, so she hurriedly hired someone from Monterey to handle the event. Justin's children were hurt and angry to be excluded. I can't blame them."

"Was there a reason she excluded them?"

"She said she didn't want to deal with sadness."

"Well, I guess it was fortunate for his kids that Justin's friends stepped up and shared those caring statements and reminiscences."

"I'm sure they appreciated that. I know I did. Justin's life deserved recognition. Shelby's behavior and poor choices are turning everyone against her. Honestly, I'm losing patience with her."

"I'm afraid I have to agree with you," said Ami.

"She's even refusing to contact the criminal attorney I recommended. She's been talking to Lucas unprotected. Oh, no offence to Lucas. I only meant that it's important for a murder suspect to have an attorney."

"Relax, Roselyn. I agree with you. An attorney is sound advice. You're right. She shouldn't be talking to the police without representation."

"Thank you for understanding. She's making things much more difficult for herself than they need to be. I can't seem to get through to her."

"What about Ethan? Do you think she would listen to him?"

"Not likely. She views him as an accommodation. She knew when she begged him to protect her, he'd respond with chivalry, but she doesn't consider him a friend. They've had, well, let's call them a few play dates."

"Can you think of anyone she might listen to?"

"Well, now that you ask. She admires Sharon. I know she'd listen to anything Sharon told her. More than once, she's mentioned wanting to be admired and powerful like Sharon." Roselyn chuckled. "Well, perhaps it's possible some day, if Shelby ever grows up. My point is, since you're good friends with Sharon, would you mind asking if she'd be willing to talk with Shelby?"

"I'd be happy to ask her. Although I'd appreciate your mentioning to Shelby that Sharon's most admirable quality is her kindness."

"Unfortunately, Shelby would view that as a weakness. So, if you don't mind, I'll hold off until after they talk."

"I promise to call Sharon and get back to you later today."

Roselyn let out a grateful sigh. "Thanks, Ami. I appreciate your help."

CHAPTER SIX

The Loss

"We've lost Kathy Riggs now," announced Josh, walking into their garden upon his return home from rehearsal.

"What do you mean by lost?" asked Bill.

"She's leaving this week for Idaho to stay with her parents for a month."

"I know it's a blow, but hardly unexpected. You said she's been missing rehearsals or crying when she does show up. Her grief over Justin has been debilitating. It's no surprise she needs to get away."

"I realize it's been painful for her and I don't want to seem uncharitable, but we open in three weeks and her leaving puts us in a bind. She's one of our strongest voices."

"The ensemble might be a little thin without her, but it's a superb musical. One less singer is not going to change that."

"I feel like all I do is rewrite for the ensemble losses."

"Surely you have an extra who can take her place?"

"We used him to fill in for Justin."

"Mary sings up a storm all day in the kitchen. Why not ask her?" suggested Bill.

"She has a fine, although untrained, voice, but she's made it very clear she is not interested in performing. Besides, we need her here."

"You're right. I'm sorry, Josh. I know this loss is difficult for you. I'll support you however you like."

"Thanks for understanding."

"Of course, mon amour."

>=<

"Hi, Roselyn, it's Ami."

"Hi, Ami."

"Sharon said she'd be happy to speak with Shelby. She's available on the seventeenth, that's a week from Friday. She'd like you and Shelby to join her for lunch at her home at noon. Would that work for both of you?"

"I'll make it work. I'd like to ask one more favor."

"What is it?"

"Neither of us knows Sharon well. You and I spent a lot a time together during the portrait and I feel comfortable with you. Is it possible for you to join us?"

"Sure. I'll be happy to join you."

"Thanks, Ami. See you then."

>=<

"Good morning, mon cher ami."

"Hi Bill, what's up?"

"I recall Marianne saying she took singing lessons. Does she sing well?"

"Yes. She has a lovely voice, strong, even. Are you asking because of the play?"

"Yes. Kathy Riggs is leaving."

"Where is she going?"

"Back home to visit her parents. She needs a change of scene to deal with her grief. I think she's doing the right thing."

"Me, too. Getting away will help her heal."

"The down side is Josh is left coping with the loss of her strong voice. Opening night is three weeks away and it's crunch time. Josh's nerves are on edge and I wanted to help. I thought I'd call Marianne to see if she was interested in filling in, but wanted to check with you on her voice quality first. It would be terrible for both her and Josh if she agreed and then sounded like a wet cat."

Ami laughed. "I promise she doesn't sound anything like that. She has a lovely voice. I'd call her."

"I will do just that."

>=<

"Hi Kathy, it's Ami."

"Do you have news about Justin's investigation?"

"Nothing yet. I'm calling because Bill mentioned you're leaving for home this week and I wanted to wish you well."

"Thanks. I'm flying out tomorrow morning, but I'll have my cell if you need to call me."

"Are you flying out of Monterey?"

"Yes."

"I'm driving to Monterey tomorrow morning to visit my mother. I could drive you to the airport."

"My friend was going to drive me, but I'm sure she'd be happy not to make the trip."

"Good. The drive will give us a chance to talk. There are a few things I'm hoping you can help us with."

"And I can tell you about something I remembered that I think might be connected."

"We'll exchange ideas on the way. What time do you want me to pick you up?"

>=<

"Hi, Mom! It's Ami. I'm driving someone to Monterey airport tomorrow morning and wondered if you have time for lunch before I head back."

"Ami, your timing couldn't be more perfect. I was just about to call you. I have some sad news."

"What is it, Mom?"

"Marianne had a miscarriage."

"Oh, I'm so sorry. Is she okay?"

"Physically, she's fine. Emotionally, she's shut down. She won't talk to anyone, which, as you know, is totally unlike her. Mike is beside himself. His efforts to be supportive continue to backfire. He has no idea how to cope with her. Knowing how close you and Marianne are, we want you to come and stay with them for a few days. We're hoping you can get her to open up."

"Let Mike know I'll be there by noon tomorrow."

"Thanks, Darling. I know Mike will be relieved you're coming."

>=<

"There's little traffic. You'll have plenty of time before boarding," said Ami.

"Good. I hate rushing."

"Me, too," Ami agreed. "So, what was it that you remembered, Kathy?"

"Shelby might not be the only one who could have poisoned Justin," informed Kathy. "Even though," she added, raising her voice with anger, "she's a heartless she-devil. I was livid to see Ethan by her side. That was deliberately cruel and disrespectful."

"I agree that was in poor taste. What changed your mind about her poisoning Justin?"

"I haven't changed my mind. She probably did it. But after calming down and reflecting on everything, two things came to mind that bother me. The first is what Justin did when he had his heart attack."

"What was that?"

"He reached out his left arm and pointed toward the fireplace. I wonder now if maybe he was trying to tell us something. It was just for a moment. Then, he grabbed his chest with his right hand and fell to the floor."

"Was anyone standing by the fireplace?" asked Ami.

85

"No."

"Then, maybe his message had something to do with the fireplace. Let's see, the portrait of Elise is there. What else?" asked Ami.

"There's a vase of orchids. And the large mirror above the fireplace," answered Kathy.

"So the possibilities are either Justin was telling you Elise poisoned him or he was pointing to someone's reflection in the mirror. Who was reflected in the mirror?"

"I don't know. I was focused on Justin. It all happened so fast."

"Do you remember who was standing across from the mirror that could have been reflected in it?"

"Most of the cast and some of the crew. The mirror is upstage left."

"I'll check at the theater if anyone else noticed. What was the second thing?"

"The day before he died, Justin mentioned receiving confirmation from his attorney about someone."

"Who?"

"He wouldn't tell me. But whoever it was, he was surprised by their behavior. He said he wouldn't have believed the person was that devious if he hadn't checked it out himself. He said he confronted the person and called him a parasite for treating a woman that way."

"Did he say what he confronted this person about?"

"No, but it had something to do with Shelby. He said the person would have gotten away with it if it hadn't been for his plans for Shelby's birthday."

"When is that?"

"It was last month."

"Did you get a chance to see that note from Justin's attorney?"

"No. But it was a text, so it should still be on his phone, which I'm guessing the police have seized. Check with Lucas."

"Can you remember anything else Justin said about the text or this person?"

"No. That's all I know. I thought it might be connected somehow to his murder. He was so brave to confront this person for Shelby. And he was so forgiving of her. Do you know, the morning he died, he told his lawyer not to hold her to the prenup financial settlement. He said he wanted his freedom, not her money. He was such a good man." Kathy pulled a tissue out of her purse and blotted her eyes.

"Did his attorney notify Shelby of this?"

"I doubt it. Justin died, so the divorce papers were never served. Shelby's motive still stands. As far as she knew, Justin was going to divorce her and she was going to have to pay up."

>=<

Ami found Marianne in bed in a darkened room.

"Hello, Dear," she greeted, cheerily.

Marianne didn't answer.

"It's good to see you're resting. Let's get some light in here." Ami walked over to pull up the blinds, but found no cord. "How do these work?"

Marianne still didn't answer.

Ami walked over and opened the bedroom door. "Mike, can you come and show me how to open the blinds?"

Mike arrived within seconds. He whispered, "They're voice activated. You say, 'Blinds up, down, tilt or close' to control them."

Ami motioned for him to raise the blinds.

"Blinds up," he voiced and the blinds rose.

As light filled the room, Marianne pulled the sheet over her head.

"Too bright, Mike. Please adjust them."

87

"Blinds down. Blinds tilt," commanded Mike.

The blinds lowered, the slats tilted and light filtered into the room more comfortably.

Mike looked over at Marianne, whose head was still covered with the sheet, and back at Ami.

"It will be okay, Dear," Ami whispered to Mike. "Leave us for a little bit."

Mike nodded and left the room.

"Marianne, I was hoping you would talk with me."

Marianne didn't answer.

"At least let me look at you," said Ami, pulling the sheet off Marianne's head. "That's better."

Marianne closed her eyes tightly.

Ami sat on the edge of bed and gave Marianne a hug. "I know this is a difficult time for you," sympathized Ami.

Marianne didn't answer. Her eyes remained closed.

Ami sat upright. "I have something to tell you and I need you to look at me."

Marianne didn't open her eyes.

"Now, Marianne," ordered Ami.

Marianne opened her eyes, blinked a few times and settled them on her aunt's face.

"I'm going to share something very few people know. I, too, had a miscarriage."

Marianne's eyes widened with surprise.

"It was in my senior year of college. Shirley was a toddler. Uncle George and I were thrilled Shirley would have a little brother or sister. Of course, it was a busy time for us, what with working part time jobs, studying for exams and running around after Shirley, but we were managing it all. I was young and healthy and felt great. Suddenly, I miscarried at eight weeks."

Tears ran down Marianne's face, but she didn't speak.

"Losing the baby was heartbreaking. George tried to be supportive, but he didn't know what to do to help me. He wanted to fix it and make it better, but you can't fix a person. Of course, he was grieving the loss, too, but his was different from mine. Mine was more personal. And I was suffering from more than grief. I was suffering from guilt."

Marianne began to cry harder and turned her head away.

"You see, I blamed myself for the miscarriage. I tortured myself with questions. Maybe if I hadn't studied so late into the night, or hadn't worked those overtime shifts or hadn't twisted so hard when I picked up Shirley? Finally, I realized I could question myself for the rest of my life and would never have an answer. Blaming myself didn't change what had happened. So, I decided to let go of my guilt and stop hurting myself, George and Shirley. Look at me, Marianne."

Ami waited until Marianne's eyes met hers.

"It's important for you to realize that questioning and blaming yourself serves no good purpose and is hurting both you and Mike. The truth is simple. This baby was not meant to be. No blame. No punishment. No guilt. Do you understand?"

Marianne let out a cry of anguish and threw herself into Ami's arms.

Within seconds, Mike flung open the door and ran into the room.

"She's okay, Mike. She's releasing. I'll be out in a little while."

He nodded and left the room, closing the door gently.

Ami rocked Marianne in her arms. Neither spoke. Eventually, Marianne quieted.

"Sleep now, Dear," purred Ami, lovingly. "I'll be back later to check on you." She got up from the bed and gathered the sheet around Marianne's shoulders. "Blinds close," she commanded to the window. As she saw the slats tightening, she left the room, closing the door behind her.

Mike was sitting on a stool at the counter, drinking a cup of coffee. He looked up with an anxious expression when Ami entered the kitchen.

"She's sleeping. She's going to be okay," assured Ami.

"Thank you." He put his hands over his face and began to sob.

Ami walked up behind him and gently rubbed his back. "I'm here for you, too, Mike. I know this has been difficult. You're dealing with your own grief and you've been worried about Marianne. It's good to release. Let it all go."

After a few minutes, Mike wiped the tears from his face with his hand. He pulled a tissue from the box on the counter and blew his nose. "I've been so worried about her. She wouldn't talk to me. Have you ever known her not to talk? I even opened champagne, you know, how she likes when she's sad? She didn't want it. I didn't know what to do. I didn't know how to help her."

"She's been suffering from grief and guilt. She blames herself for the miscarriage."

"Why? It wasn't her fault. She did everything the doctor suggested. She took the supplements, followed the diet, did the exercises."

"It's not uncommon for women to blame themselves when they have a miscarriage. Their active, busy lives don't stop when they find out they're pregnant, so they often blame themselves for overdoing it."

"You mean Marianne blames herself over all the activity with the new house?" realized Mike.

"Yes."

"So, how do I help her?"

"Be what you always are, patient and supportive. Let her talk about it when she wants. It'll take her a little while to work through her grief and guilt, but she has a resilient nature. It's going to be okay, Mike."

>=<

"I assume Marianne is feeling better since your visit," offered Bill. He had invited Ami for lunch upon her return home.

"Yes. She'll need some time to process the loss, but she's rebounding fairly quickly to daily function."

"I'm happy to hear it. And I'm glad I changed my mind about calling her to sing. I would have hated the thought I'd caused additional stress. I'd love to talk with her. Do you think she's up to it?"

"She was chatting about accessories for their guest room before I left. I'm sure she'd love to discuss that with you."

"I'm relieved to hear she's talking again. I found her silence concerning. She's normally such a chatterbox."

"We all did," agreed Ami. "She started talking a little bit the day after I arrived which was a great relief to Mike. She's almost up to full speed now."

"Good. I'll give her a call tomorrow."

"She'll enjoy that. I gather Josh is still busy with rehearsals."

"He's dealing with tech rehearsals this week. They're always time consuming and tedious.'"

"I'm sure he's feeling stressed."

"He's been on edge. We're being gentle with him."

"Was he able to get more singers?" asked Ami.

"Elise came to the rescue by getting Lou to join the ensemble. He's not a trained singer, but he has a strong, even voice and since he participates in the holiday chorus each year, he has experience singing with a group. He'll fill in nicely. Elise is working with him at home to get him up to speed. By the way, she's the happiest I've ever seen her. She said they've created a comfortable love nest. She even mentioned marriage may be in their future."

"Really? That's wonderful!"

"I think seeing you and Lucas so committed was the little nudge she needed. Are you happy, mon cher ami?"

Ami smiled broadly. "Yes, Bill, I'm very happy."

"Aah, l'amour est merveilleux," sighed Bill. "Now, on to gossip. I heard you're having lunch with Shelby and Roselyn tomorrow. Mind telling me what that's about."

"What? Your informant didn't tell you our agenda?"

"No, but I'm assuming you plan to question her as part of your investigation."

"The lunch is a favor for Roselyn. She's hoping Sharon can talk some sense into Shelby."

"I didn't realize Sharon performed miracles."

"Seriously, Bill, Roselyn is worried about Shelby not making good choices and giving the impression she isn't grieving Justin."

"Certainly the impression I got."

"Also, since most of the community assumes Shelby is guilty, Roselyn is hoping Sharon can provide some advice on how Shelby can gain back support."

"Afraid that train has left the station. What's happening with your investigation? Any suspects besides Shelby?"

"No real evidence on anyone. I'm hoping more conversations with more people will lead to something tangible. Did Justin mention anything to you about a confrontation with someone? It may have had something to do with Shelby's birthday."

"No. He never mentioned anything like that to me."

"He mentioned it to Kathy. She said he confirmed something with his attorney and seemed surprised by the person's deceitful behavior. It made him angry and he confronted the person and called him a parasite. He didn't tell her who the person was, but said he would have gotten away with it if it hadn't been for Shelby's birthday. Did he mention anything to you about being angry with someone?"

"No, but he wouldn't have trusted me to hold my tongue over something so juicy."

"Would he have confided in someone other than you or Kathy?"

"No," stated Bill, firmly.

"Another thing Kathy mentioned was that on the morning he was poisoned, Justin told his attorney not to file for the prenup penalty. He told her he wanted his freedom, not Shelby's money. Did he mention anything to you about planning to do that?"

"No, he never mentioned anything to me. In fact, the only thing he trusted me with was the existence of a prenup, no details. I assume you discovered them. Give."

"Bottom line is Shelby would have had to pay Justin two million dollars if he divorced her."

"No wonder he held it from me. I would have blabbed about that. Gives Shelby a hefty motive."

"Yes. I better ask Sharon to confirm Justin's hold on the prenup penalty. Maybe something Shelby says at lunch tomorrow will be useful in moving this investigation forward."

"I'm happy you're back on the case. I hope this latest bit of information will lead to the person who killed Justin."

CHAPTER SEVEN

The Lunch

"That was a wonderful lunch. Thanks for inviting us," said Shelby, as they followed Sharon into her living room. "I know Roselyn put you up to it, but it was nice of you to go along."

"It was my pleasure. I propose we relax with a glass of champagne during our discussion." She handed them each a glass from the prepared tray and invited them to sit.

"Shelby, I understand you'd like my assistance. How can I help you?" initiated Sharon.

"Everyone thinks I killed Justin. No matter where I go, I can feel their suspicion. I can't even have lunch at the club without stares and dirty looks. It makes my skin crawl."

"I expect your reality since Justin's death has been hurtful and frightening," offered Sharon.

"Yes, it has. And it's not fair. How do I get them to stop treating me like an outcast?"

"People's suspicion of you will stop when whoever killed Justin is arrested," confirmed Ami.

"They're not investigating anyone else. They suspect me since I filled his thermos. But Roselyn was there. She saw me. I poured that herbal mess in it and nothing else. She was a witness."

"I gave a statement to the police confirming that," supported Roselyn.

"I want a normal life. I'm tired of being judged."

"Neither Ami nor I are judging you," assured Sharon.

"And we do want to help," added Ami.

"Thanks. I appreciate having someone on my side. Everyone else hates me. Especially since I brought Ethan to the celebration of life. That really backfired."

"Roselyn told me you asked Ethan to sit with you as protection. Were you afraid of somebody, Shelby?" asked Ami.

"I was afraid of everybody. I didn't want to face all those people by myself. I've always turned to men when I needed bolstering. I thought I'd feel stronger if Ethan was with me. It was a mistake. It made them hate me even more. I just made it worse."

"Much worse," murmured Roselyn.

Shelby glanced her way, with sad eyes.

"Sorry."

"Don't be. I know I've made some bad choices. I should have listened to you."

"I'm relieved you agreed to an attorney, finally," responded Roselyn.

"My attorney has been a life saver. She's relieved a lot of my fears. But it's still scary being a suspect in a murder."

"I imagine it is," sympathized Sharon.

"It's been hard." Shelby looked over at Ami. "I know you've been looking into Justin's death. Have you found anyone other than me who could have done it?"

"Not yet. I would need to know more about Justin to do that. Do you mind if I ask you a few questions?"

"I've already told Lucas everything I could think of."

"Due to police confidentiality, Lucas is unable to share with me."

"I'm not buying that," accused Shelby.

"Nevertheless, it's true."

"No pillow talk?"

"No," replied Ami.

"Ami and I work independently of the police," informed Sharon. "It allows us to collect data and ascertain motives with more objectivity."

"Oh, I see. I didn't realize that."

Ami could tell Shelby was clearly impressed by Sharon being personally involved in this investigation, and would willingly cooperate with her. Ami decided to sit back and let Sharon take the lead with Shelby.

"To that end," continued Sharon, smiling sweetly, "we would appreciate your answering Ami's questions as honestly and thoroughly as possible. Would you be willing to do that for us?"

Ami was impressed with how easily Sharon took full advantage of Shelby's admiration.

"Yes, of course. What do you want to know?"

"Money and love are the most common motives. I'd like to explore them as they relate to both you and Justin," explained Ami. "Let's start with Justin. What can you tell me about Justin and money?"

"You mean like how much did he have?"

"No. More like his spending, debts, gambling. That sort of thing."

"Justin didn't believe in debt. Well, he always used his credit card to get the rewards, but he paid it off every month. And he never gambled so that's out."

"Not even with investments?" asked Ami.

"Justin didn't believe in taking chances. He made a point of financially protecting himself. One look at our prenup would convince you of that."

"Then I assume he didn't loan others money either."

"Definitely not. Not even his kids and he loved them like crazy."

"If money is out. What about love?"

"There's Kathy Riggs," replied Shelby with a smile. "I knew what was going on."

"Are you saying Kathy and Justin had a romantic relationship?"

"I doubt it was physical. Justin was too righteous to cheat sexually, but it definitely was romantic. She was in love with him. And I believe Justin loved her, too. She's the nurturing type. That would have fitted his needs."

"Thank you for your candor. That leads us to money and love as it pertains to you." Ami tilted her head and raised an eyebrow. "Do you mind if I ask some blunt questions?"

Shelby smirked. "It's no secret I cheated on Justin. And, yes, he found out and planned to divorce me. And, yes, I would have had to pay him a pile of money. Makes suspicion kind of fall back to me, doesn't it?"

"Not necessarily," said Ami. "Were you aware that Justin instructed his attorney to relieve you of the prenup penalty?"

"No!" snapped Shelby. "Is that really true?"

Ami noted Shelby's surprise was genuine.

"Yes, it's true."

"I can't believe he did that. I just assumed since it was in the prenup, it was a done deal." She looked down at her lap. "If I had only known, but then he still..." She stopped murmuring to herself and looked up at them. "I'm surprised to hear it."

"He must have really loved you to give up all that money," said Roselyn.

"I guess so."

"So who else loved you?" asked Ami. "Justin hadn't made your impending divorce public. Is it possible one of the men you were seeing wanted Justin out of the picture?"

"Those were flings, not relationships. None of it was serious. It was all in fun."

"You considered it fun, but is it possible it was more serious for one of them?"

"None professed their love for me, if that's what you mean," scoffed Shelby.

"Which leads us back to money. You're a wealthy woman. Is it possible one of the men was after your money?"

"I doubt it. They'd have no reason to think I'd support them. In any case, finances were never mentioned during our brief time together."

"I'm assuming none asked to borrow money," suggested Roselyn.

"No. And I wouldn't have given them any if they did," shot Shelby. "I'm not that stupid."

"Before he died, Justin confirmed some information with his attorney. Based on that information, he confronted someone he felt might possibly hurt you," informed Ami. "Why would he be trying to protect you?"

Shelby moved forward in her chair. "I have no idea. I don't know anything about that."

Again, Ami easily could tell from Shelby's face she didn't have a clue.

"Are you thinking the person Justin confronted was one of Shelby's affairs?" suggested Roselyn.

"It's possible. It's also possible that confrontation was the reason Justin was poisoned."

"Do you really think Justin might have been killed for defending me?"

"Possibly."

"So, you're seriously looking at someone other than Shelby?" asked Roselyn.

"Yes."

"Well, that's a relief," piped Shelby with a smile.

"Would you be willing to provide the names of the men you were involved with?"

"Oh, Lucas has all that."

"He can't share with her, remember?" prompted Roselyn.

"Oh, right. Okay, there were four," Shelby began.

"That was enlightening," assessed Sharon, when her lunch guests had departed and she and Ami were alone.

"Congratulations on the smooth way you turned Shelby's hero worship into cooperation. You really are an expert at manipulation. Impressive!"

Sharon smiled. "It was obvious her high regard could be used to our advantage."

"Do you think Shelby was right about Justin's financial purity?"

"Yes, I do. None of my calls resulted in anything slightly questionable and they would have. Given Justin's personality, it seems unlikely that he would have engaged in under-the-table financial dealings."

"Then contacting Justin's attorney to confirm he dismissed the prenup penalty and what caused that confrontation is our next step," directed Ami.

"I shall make the call."

"Thanks. Hopefully, he'll name one of the men on Shelby's list. Did you add their names to your notes?"

"Yes. I confess her mention of David surprised me. I assumed he was gay. I am embarrassed that I succumbed to good looks and theater as my assumption," admitted Sharon.

"My shocker was Shelby naming Robby. Can't believe Shelby would do that to Roselyn. Granted they were divorced at the time of the affair, but still."

"It was distasteful," agreed Sharon.

"Yes. Which makes me curious about Robby. During one of our portrait sessions, Roselyn mentioned he divorced her to be with the love of his life. If he was so in love with this new woman, why was he having an affair with Shelby?"

"Bill can provide you far more detail. However, it is widely known that once Robby divorced Roselyn, the love of his life, Terese, soon parted ways with him. Affairs are ethereal. Relationships are reality," observed Sharon.

"Roselyn didn't seem a bit surprised when Shelby gave us his name, so she must have been aware of their fling. Still, I detected a bit of anger in her eyes," noted Ami.

"Reasonable. I would expect even an ex to be deemed personal property."

"And then there's Roger. I'm interested in the timing and overlap of his relationship with Kathy, her friendship with Justin and his liaison with Shelby."

"No doubt Bill can provide you with a time line."

"Of the four, David and Roger are our most likely suspects since they were at rehearsal with Justin that day," said Ami.

"Robby would have been present as well," corrected Sharon.

"At the theater?"

"Yes. Robby is part of the ensemble."

"Was he there during our tour?"

"Yes."

"Do you realize today's lunch has produced three suspects who would have had access to Justin's thermos?" declared Ami.

>=<

"How was your lunch today? Uncover anything I should know?" asked Lucas as they sat on the deck before dinner.

"According to Shelby, she's already informed you. It was all new to me since I have a husband who is stingy about sharing."

"Maybe she hasn't told me everything. It's possible you found out something I don't know. Want to share?"

"Will you share back?"

100

"Can't promise that."

"Well, since I want to talk about it, I'll tell you. I found out David, Roger and Robby were at the theater the day Justin was poisoned and Shelby had affairs with all of them."

"I assumed Sharon will be checking out their finances."

"Yes. And I assume you already have."

"No comment."

"Sharon said she was surprised when Shelby mentioned David."

"Why?"

"She assumed he was gay."

"Not gay. Very popular with the ladies," informed Lucas.

"Easy to believe. He's exceptionally handsome and he has that hint of an accent. Is it French or Italian?"

"Italian."

"And although he doesn't flaunt it, he possesses that film star sex appeal. I'm surprised Sharon wasn't aware of his stud status. Do you think she was lying to me?"

"No, I don't think she was lying. Unlike Bill, Sharon doesn't inquire into people's love lives. Her only contact with David is at the theater. She doesn't socialize with him. He's not a member of her private circle."

"We are a rather elite group. Happenstance and crime got me in. How about you?"

"Arthur took a shine to me."

"Well, aren't we special," fancied Ami.

Lucas laughed.

"Outrageous wealth aside, Sharon really is a kind and generous person," defended Ami.

"I genuinely like Arthur, too."

"Do you know what creeped me out today?"

"What?" asked Lucas with interest.

"Roselyn's ex on Shelby's list. You'd think Shelby would be a little more considerate of her best friend."

"Well, if she wasn't considerate of her husband, it's not surprising she wasn't considerate of Roselyn."

"Roselyn didn't act surprised when Shelby mentioned his name, but I noticed a touch of anger in her eyes."

"It's understandable she'd object to her friend hooking up with her ex. All of this is old news. Got anything you think I don't already know?"

"You realize we could save a lot of time by joining forces."

"I thought we had."

"It's a one way exchange. I give and you take."

"I think our system works best for all concerned."

"I can see where you'd think so," confronted Ami.

"Seriously, not knowing anything the police are tracking allows you to question from a fresh perspective. You're looking at this with an open mind. You have the opportunity to discover something we missed. You view a piece of information in a different light and through your own filter. Most importantly, people will tell you things they won't admit to me."

"Sounds like you're using me as unpaid help."

"Let's consider it a marital side benefit."

Ami stuck her tongue out at him.

"Your childishness aside, you must realize how much I admire you."

"Keep talking."

"You have a logical mind with solid investigative skills. I trust and appreciate the information you provide."

She smiled at him. "Thank you. In that case, I will proceed with my own investigation and report on my progress."

He leaned over and kissed her. "All I ask is that you be careful. If you show up dead, it would complicate my investigation."

"Oh, Ami, the painting seems even more beautiful now that it's dried!" said Roselyn unwrapping it.

"I'm so happy you're pleased."

"Come. Let me show you where I'm going to hang it." She led Ami to the library and pointed to a space on a wall between two tall book shelves. "What do you think?"

"I think it's perfect."

"Now, I'm with the rest," Roselyn nodded with satisfaction toward the other portraits around the room.

"I'm assuming these are other family members."

"Yes, parents, grandparents, great-grandparents, etc."

"This is a beautiful and impressive library. There must be well over a hundred books here," admired Ami, glancing across the shelves.

"Three hundred and fifty-two to be exact. And my father read every one of them. He had them cataloged. Almost a third are first editions. He loved spending time in this room. That's him over there." Roselyn pointed across the room to the portrait of a man with wavy white hair.

"He has strong, even features and you have his smile. He's a handsome man."

"Yes, he was. He died last year of a heart attack. It was sudden and unexpected."

"I'm sorry you lost your father. I don't remember your mentioning it to me."

"It's hard for me to talk about. I'm still recovering. Odd little things can bring me to tears. Once, it was someone wearing a sweater similar to his favorite. Another time, it was a white haired guest at the club. It's silly, really."

"It's understandable you would have these feelings. The death of a parent is a deep loss."

"I suppose it's orphan syndrome. My mother died a number of years ago."

"So, that leaves you and your older sister. I believe you told me she joined a convent when she was young. Are you able to keep in touch?"

"Yes. We manage weekly video chats and she visits at Christmas. We're close, but it's not like we can hang out."

"You and Shelby seem close, too."

"Shelby has limitations when it comes to friendship. She's immature and self-centered and, unfortunately, impulsive. Our relationship is more caretaking than friendship; she's like the unruly freshman and I'm the house mother. I don't mind. I think she needs protecting."

"That's really kind of you. Roselyn, I've been curious about something ever since our lunch at Sharon's. I hope you won't be offended if I ask a personal question."

"I think I can guess. How do I feel about Shelby and my ex-husband hooking up?"

"Yes," confirmed Ami.

"Oh, I suppose there's a little part of me that resents it, but the truth is it's none of my business. Robby and I were divorced when it happened. He was free to sleep with anyone he wanted. I suppose you could say he felt free throughout our marriage. Shelby considers their fling 'an accident.'" Roselyn chuckled. "Typical Shelby."

"What did she mean by accident?"

"That it wasn't her fault. Her excuse was they both had way too much to drink at Gail Fielding's brunch and it just happened."

"Oh, I see."

"For all her quirks, she values my friendship. She was worried about losing me, so she made a point to tell me the next day, before I could hear it from someone else, and begged my forgiveness."

"And you immediately forgave her?"

"Yes, to comfort her. Secretly, I was still angry about it. After a few days, it occurred to me how lucky I was Robby was no longer my problem, and the anger faded away."

"I hope Shelby realizes how fortunate she is to have you as a friend."

"I'm not sure she does. But she really appreciated the lunch the other day with you and Sharon. It buoyed her spirits to think someone wanted to help her. And she's relieved you're investigating another suspect. I know it's soon, but were you able to find out anything?"

"We're still checking. No answers yet. These types of inquiries tend to take patience."

"I suppose they do. If there's anything I can do to help, please let me know. I'd be happy to make inquiries or research information or assist however you need," offered Roselyn.

"I might take you up on that."

"Before you leave, I'd love for you to join me in the garden for tea. Do you have time?" invited Roselyn.

"Oh, I'd enjoy that. Thank you."

Roselyn led Ami out to a table nestled in a garden of rose bushes.

"Make yourself comfortable and I'll get the tea."

Ami sat in a comfortably padded chair at the table and admired the roses surrounding her. The pink roses nearby had a familiar scent, although it wasn't rose. She sniffed the air a couple of times and realized they smelled like raspberries.

Roselyn returned with a tea tray and set it on the table. She poured Ami a cup and handed it to her. Then, she passed Ami a plate of petit fours.

"Thank you.   I was sitting here enjoying the fragrance of these pink roses. Surprisingly, they smell like raspberries."

"Yes, they're an heirloom my mother planted. She wanted a rose compatible to tea service."

"She succeeded. It's yummy," complimented Ami.

"As a child, I'd sit between the bushes, enjoying the fragrance, while my mother and her friends sat nearby having tea. Mother adored roses. Her name was Rose and she named my sister Rosemae and me Roselyn so that pretty much says it all."

"Your garden is beautiful. You have a lovely variety."

"This rose garden is a family tradition, from my three times great grandmother to, now, me. Every generation adds their favorite. My contribution are the white rose bushes by the garden entrance. It's a hybrid my gardening club helped me create. I named it for my mother, The Cabrillo Rose."

"I didn't realize you did the gardening yourself. I assumed you hired someone to do it all. It must be a lot of work for you."

"I have a service that maintains the grounds and most of the gardens. My focus is the roses. When I'm out here working, I feel connected to all of the women in my family."

"I'm sure that's enjoyable and comforting for you. I admire you and your gardening friends creating a hybrid rose. That sounds like a difficult project."

"Hybrids aren't difficult. They just take patience. After several tries at pollination failed, we found success with grafting. The other gardeners were really supportive. They're great friends. I'm grateful for them."

"I'm surprised you never mentioned your rose garden during our time together. It's obviously important to you."

"Over the years, I've learned that passionate gardeners make people's eyes glaze over." She laughed. "So, I mostly talk about it with fellow gardeners."

"Is Bill a member of your gardening group?"

"Bill's too professional for us. He's been a guest speaker a couple of times and he's given us an enjoyable tour of his garden. It's a magical place."

"Magical is what my mother called it, too. She recently had an opportunity to visit. Both your garden and home are beautiful, Roselyn. Living here must be very enjoyable for you."

"It is. Except for when I was at college, I've lived here all my life. My father deeded me this house as a wedding gift. He moved out to give us privacy. I tried to get him to stay, but he insisted on moving into a condo at the club. He joined us for meals about once a week. After Robby and I divorced, Father finally agreed to move back. By then, his eyesight was very weak. He could no longer read, but he still spent most of his day in his library listening to audio books. I used to join him there for tea."

"I'm sure you treasure that time together."

"I have some wonderful memories. Now, I enjoy living alone and having the house all to myself."

"I can barely keep my tiny beach house clean. How do you manage this large house all alone?"

"Oh, I have weekly gardening, cleaning and food delivery services. Mother and Father had live-in help, but it was what they were used to and they entertained a lot. I rarely entertain. Most nights, I meet friends at the club for dinner. I think people often confuse being alone with being lonely. I don't feel at all lonely."

"I know what you mean and agree with you. I think it takes a secure person to enjoy her own company. You sound like you've found peace, Roselyn."

"Yes, I have."

"I have thoroughly enjoyed our visit and now I need to be on my way. Thank you so much for sharing your garden with me."

"You're welcome. I meant what I said about calling if you want my help."

"I will keep that in mind. I can see how your reasonable disposition and logical mind could be valuable."

CHAPTER EIGHT

The Secret

"I forgot how cozy and comfortable your house is, Aunt Ami. I fell in love with it the minute I saw those photos on your phone. I said it was perfect for you. Remember?"

"Of course, I do, Dear. I also remember how supportive you were of my move and all of the effort you put into the decor. I appreciate that."

"Now, it's perfect for both of you. Was it hard to give up your house and move in here, Uncle Lucas?"

"Not at all. I'm partial to this deck. It's the first place I head when I come home from work." He placed the steaks on the table. "Dig in."

"Smells wonderful. I was craving steak today and here it is! Thanks for inviting us to dinner."

"It's our pleasure, Dear."

"Mike's like you, Uncle Lucas. He sits out on our deck before dinner almost every evening. Don't you?"

"It helps me unwind," said Mike. "I think it's the waves. The movement and the sound seem to wash all my cares away."

"For me, it's the vastness," said Lucas. "You look out to a giant mass of water. Makes the irritations of the day seem small and unimportant."

"Wow! I had no idea you two were so philosophical."

"We're more than pretty faces," declared Mike.

"Yeah," added Lucas.

Marianne laughed. "Oh, please! By the way, what are we having for dessert, Aunt Ami?"

"We've barely started dinner, Dear."

"I know, but steak is filling and I need to know how much room to leave."

"I made those fresh cherry brownies you like."

"Ooh, yummy! I want more than one of those." She cut off a piece of her steak and transferred it Mike's plate. "There! Now I'll have more room for brownies."

"As you can see, she uses me as her dumpster. I welcome the steak, but yesterday, she tried to turn my office into her overflow closet," complained Mike.

Marianne rolled her eyes. "Exaggeration. I added a few accessories and he threw a fit and made me take them away."

"I prefer my office unencumbered. It's organized and efficient."

"But it doesn't have any flare."

"Any flare needs to suit Mike, not you," chided Ami.

"Thanks, and well said, Aunt Ami! Bill agrees, too. He said he has a few ideas he'll go over with me when he comes to work with Marianne next week."

"You talked with Bill?" accused Marianne.

"Yes. You do realize he doesn't belong to you."
Ami laughed.

"Why are you laughing?"

"Because he's right. You tend to be possessive."

Marianne raised her head haughtily. "I'm not going to dignify that with a response. Mike, tell them how great your business is going."

"It's going better than expected. I thought it'd be slow for awhile, but I have a number of clients already."

"I assume you're enjoying being your own boss," said Lucas.

"Yes. I'm finally scheduling my time at a pace that allows me to enjoy my work."

"His office is clear across the house so I won't interrupt him. Sometimes, I just happen to wander over there. But I haven't bothered him at all this week because I started working on a new game. Other than programming the house, I hadn't work in awhile, so it feels good to get back to it."

"I heard about those voice activated blinds of yours," said Lucas.

"I kind of went on a programming spree and now just about everything in our house is voice activated."

"How do you feel about that, Mike?" asked Ami.

"I don't mind. It's convenient."

Ami smiled at Marianne. "It's wonderful you're working again, Dear. I'm happy for you."

"Me, too. It feels great! Oh, by the way, my distributor doesn't want anyone to know I have a new game coming out. They're afraid sales may drop on my current one. So keep it secret. Okay?"

"I promise not to mention it. So, besides working with Mike on his office, what will Bill be doing next week?" asked Ami.

"Accessories. Initially, I wanted him to help me turn the nursery into a guest room, but he suggested we focus on finishing the accessories before making any changes. I've been trying to sort out all I bought, but I keep changing my mind about which rooms I want to put stuff in."

"I'm sure the two of you will have a lot of fun sorting it out."

"Yeah, we will. And it's thanks to you and Uncle Lucas that he's coming so soon. He was going to wait until after Justin's murder was solved, but he said since your moving slow, he'll come next week. So, tell me about your investigation collaboration."

"It's pretty much like your home offices. We each have our own space," said Ami. "I assume Bill told you all about the murder and what we've discovered so far?"

"He said Justin had a heart attack from an overdose of potassium and that his wife, Shelby, is the main suspect with both motive and opportunity. Bill can't believe you haven't arrested her yet, Uncle Lucas. He said he's running out of patience with you."

"Is he?"

"Yes. Is it true you're looking into some person that Justin confronted, Aunt Ami?"

"Yes."

"Bill thinks that's a dead end."

"Why's he think that?"

"He said it's more logical Justin was killed by someone who had easy access to his food and no one had better access than Shelby. It makes sense. Most of the time, it's the spouse who did it, you know."

"I've heard that," agreed Lucas with a smile.

"Oh, don't even try being cute with me unless you plan to take me on," challenged Marianne.

"Fair enough," conceded Lucas. "I was going to ask you your thoughts, but it sounds like you're siding with Bill that Shelby did it."

"Yeah, I am. Sorry, Aunt Ami."

"I'm not offended."

"What about you, Uncle Lucas? Why don't you tell us who you think did it?"

"I'm wondering if there's a third option."

"Like what?" eagerly asked Marianne.

"I'd like you to provide one."

"I don't have any facts. How do you expect me to come up with something?"

"Anyone who can create multi-level games has the ability to come up with plenty of ideas. What do you think could be a third option?"

"Okay, let me think." Marianne was quiet for a few minutes, then smiled at him. "Revenge! My guess is Justin hurt somebody and they got back at him."

Lucas smiled back at her.

Marianne's face brightened. "I'm right, aren't I?"

"Why don't you take it out for a spin? Ask Bill."

"Lucas is right. Bill knew Justin better than anyone. We should ask him if he's aware of any incident where Justin may have hurt someone."

"You can ask him if you want, Aunt Ami, but Bill's answer is immaterial."

"Why?" asked Ami.

"Because it doesn't matter if Justin is even aware of hurting someone for revenge to work as an option. A hurt person wants to get back at Justin for whatever reason, comes up with a plan and kills him. Done."

>=<

"Hi Ami, it's Shelby."

"Hello, Shelby. What can I do for you?"

"Do you have some time to meet with me this afternoon? I won't keep you long. I have something important I need to tell you."

"How about two o'clock? Do you know where I live?"

"Roselyn gave me your address. Only, would it be okay if I asked her to come along? I don't know if I can do this without moral support."

"Of course."

"And one more thing. Can you make sure Sharon isn't there? I'd be too embarrassed to confess this in front of her. I couldn't take her disappointment in me."

Ami smiled at Shelby's wanting to save face with Sharon, but having no fear of disappointing Ami.

"I understand. I'll see you both at two."

>=<

"You have a great view," complimented Shelby, standing on Ami's deck.

"Yes, spending time out here brings me a lot of enjoyment," responded Ami, setting the tray with coffee and cake on the table. Sitting, she asked. "So, Shelby, what is it you came to tell me?"

"You said Justin confronted someone to protect me. I've been thinking about that and I think someone might have found out my dirty little secret."

"Is it something they could use as blackmail?" asked Ami.

"Yes," admitted Shelby. "It's something shameful." She stopped to stir sugar into her coffee. She raised her head to Ami. "I've never confessed this to anyone before."

"I promise not to judge you."

"Okay, here goes." Shelby took a deep breath. "After I graduated from college, I went back home and my parents supported me. For appearances sake, and to give me something to do, my father asked Jon Aubel to hire me to work in his gallery. He agreed because my father was one of his best clients and because he only had to pay me commissions. Turns out, my youth and looks attracted male clients to the gallery. And my flirting increased sales. Within a few months, I was making commissions." Shelby stopped talking and slowly took a sip of coffee.

"Is that your secret? You flirted with men to make sales?" asked Roselyn.

"Of course, not," snapped Shelby. She took another deep breath. "I enjoyed working with Jon Aubel and learning about art.   He was twice my age, but he was handsome and sexy. I fell madly in love with him. We began an intense affair. I'd never felt that kind of passion before...or since." She offered them an ironic smile. "After a few months, his wife found out and he ended our affair and fired me. I was crushed." She shook her head sadly. "I couldn't believe he chose her over me. I thought he loved me as much as I loved him. I had pictured us running off together. I was heartbroken and angry." Shelby stopped to take another breath before resuming. "So, that night, I went back to the gallery and broke in."

"Broke in! What about the alarms and the guards?"

"It was a tiny gallery, Roselyn, not some museum. I worked there. I had the alarm code. Can I continue now?"

"Of course," replied Roselyn.

"Long story short, I broke in, ripped his favorite painting off the wall, ran home and hid it under my bed."

"Surely, he would have noticed it was missing and assumed it was you. Did he confront you?" asked Roselyn.

"No. I never saw him again. The maid found the painting the next morning when she was cleaning. When my mother questioned me, I confessed the affair and the theft. I think she had guessed about the affair. I was a crying mess. She told my father. He went to the gallery and paid for the painting. He didn't mention the affair to Jon, but he never bought art from him again."

"If your father paid for the painting, what's the problem?" asked Roselyn.

"The problem is I broke into a gallery and stole a painting. What if this is why Justin was defending me?" She turned from Roselyn to Ami. "I want to tell my lawyer so that person can be another suspect, but I'm afraid if I do, I'll get arrested for theft."

Ami had listened quietly and had studied Shelby intently through her recollections. She believed Shelby's story. Her emotion as a somewhat naïve and spurned young girl had genuinely reflected in her eyes and face.

"I suggest we review this logically," proposed Ami. "Initially, stealing the painting was theft. Rather than file a report with the police, Jon Aubel chose to accept your father's payment. The gallery was a private business. More than likely, he recorded it as a sale. Therefore, your theft of the painting was settled as a private business transaction. It was no longer criminal."

"You mean I can't be arrested?"

"I have no idea what the statute of limitation is on breaking into a gallery, but it seems highly unlikely that Jon would go to the police after all these years. Don't you agree?"

"He can't. Jon died of cancer last year. I cried for days when I heard."

"It's obvious you loved him very much," said Ami.

"All my life. I've never loved anyone like I loved him."

"Is that what all the affairs are about? You do realize you can't recreate that love," counseled Roselyn.

"Oh, let it go. We're talking about the theft. Even if it's not a crime anymore, what if someone was trying to blackmail Justin about it?"

"This isn't the reason for Justin's death," objected Roselyn.

"How do you know?" challenged Shelby.

"Because it makes no sense."

"I came here for Ami's advice, not yours."

"Roselyn has a point to make. Let's hear her out," said Ami.

"I think it's highly unlikely that someone heard about and used the theft to blackmail Justin," continued Roselyn. "But even if someone did, what would be the point in killing him? You kill the blackmailer, not the person paying the blackmail. If Justin was killed for trying to protect Shelby, it wasn't over something that happened in the past. It was about something that was happening now."

CHAPTER NINE

The Suspects

"I don't understand why Shelby hasn't been arrested yet," complained Bill. "I'm disappointed by how long all of this is taking."

"I'm sorry, Bill, but the police need evidence to arrest someone," reminded Ami.

"Shelby is the one who prepared his thermos."

"That doesn't prove she put the potassium in it. And Roselyn made a police statement that she was present and didn't see Shelby put anything in but his herbal coffee."

"Shelby could have put the potassium in the thermos before Roselyn got there."

"That's true, and it's possible she did exactly that, but the police have to prove it. What they really need is some forensic type of evidence, like DNA, that will hold up in court."

"Lucas should confront Shelby and make her confess."

"Come on, Bill, be serious. You know Lucas doesn't strong arm people. Why is the delay upsetting you?"

"Because Justin is being forgotten. After he died, he was all anyone could talk about. Now, they act like he never existed. I don't want Justin to be forgotten and his murder to go unsolved."

"I promise you Lucas will not let this go unsolved. Besides, I'm beginning to doubt that Shelby is capable of planning a murder."

"What do you mean?"

"The more interaction I have with her, the more I'm convinced she doesn't have the initiative or discipline to have researched and planned something like this."

Bill sat quietly thinking for a moment before admitting, "I have to agree. Shelby's not stupid, but she's lazy and lacks self-control. I doubt she'd make the effort. Still, she's the one who filled the thermos."

"She's not the only one who had access to that thermos. It was sitting on the break room table all day. Kathy noticed it went missing which means there's a good chance someone in the theater put the potassium in there and then took the thermos away. Hopefully, the police have recovered it. I think it's time to widen our scope of suspects. Tell me about David Carson, Robby Kelly and Roger Swanson."

"Why do you want to know about them?"

"Because they were at the theater that day and they all had affairs with Shelby. Justin may have confronted any of them. If so, can you think of any reason he would have needed to protect Shelby from them?"

"Not really. She initiated the affairs so no need for protection there. And there was no reason for a jealous confrontation. Justin's attorney was ready to serve the divorce papers. Shelby would be out of his life and he would move on, probably with Kathy."

"I agree it wasn't jealousy about the affairs. Kathy said Justin had confirmed something about the person before the confrontation. He mentioned a connection with Shelby's birthday and called the person a parasite for treating a woman that way. What could he have found out about David, Robby or Roger that would warrant the word parasite?"

"Their relationships with Shelby were limited to hook ups, so I guess you could call them womanizers. But they weren't leading Shelby on. She wanted a fling, not a relationship. She wasn't a victim. There'd be no reason for Justin to confront any of them about treating her badly or calling him a parasite."

"I agree. Tell me about Robby's other affairs. I was told he had a long term affair with Terese, the love of his life, and divorced Roselyn to be with her. Was that his only affair during their marriage?"

"He engaged in numerous affairs before, during and after his marriage."

"Is it true he left Roselyn for Terese?"

"To be accurate, Roselyn confronted him and tossed him out. He immediately moved in with Terese. Shortly thereafter, Terese inharmoniously facilitated his departure."

"Why?"

"Terese found out about his histoire d'amour with Lily."

"Is he with Lily now?"

"No. After Terese threw him out, he sheltered with Lily, briefly, while he was closing on his condo."

"When did he have the affair with Shelby?"

"Post Lily," informed Bill.

"Okay, let's move on to David. Tell me about his cheating history."

"David doesn't cheat because he never commits. He has no intention of coupling and is up-front about that. He prefers intelligent, attractive women occupied with their own interests. He never lacks for companionship because he's an enjoyably generous companion," enlightened Bill with a grin.

"Point taken," chuckled Ami. "What's the story on Roger?"

"Basically, a one-woman-at-a-time kind of guy. I believe he was in love with Kathy and hurt by her friendship with Justin."

"Is that the reason he cheated on Kathy with Shelby?"

"He didn't cheat. The affair with Shelby, which she went out of her social circle to initiate, followed Kathy's break up with him. My personal opinion is Shelby had the affair with Roger to get back at Justin for his close friendship with Kathy. It would be like her to be mesquin comme ça."

"Okay, let's move on to the three of them and money. Shelby is wealthy. So, maybe one of them wanted her money. We'll start with Robby. He married Roselyn and she's wealthy. Were Terese and Lily wealthy?"

"Wealth is relative, of course. It'd be easier for me to group our community into categories. Alone at the top is Sharon. Her fortune runs into billions. Next, we have the family inheritance set, with varying fortunes in the millions. It includes Arthur, Roselyn, Shelby, etc. Terese falls into that category. Then, we have the non-inheritance, million dollar group. These are either self-made or married into. Lily is a widow there. And finally, we have the remaining ninety percent of our community folk who, like you and me, continue to toil for our daily bread, all with various income levels," concluded Bill.

"I see your point. So, back to Robby. He married into Roselyn's inherited millions, but, personally, did he inherit or is he self-made?"

"Both. Robby was a jeweler by profession and owned a successful business in Sacramento. He sold his business to pursue a life of leisure, after receiving a large endowment upon his father's death. His family is new money so he has an ego about it. Shortly thereafter, he married Roselyn, who comes from old money. He was particularly impressed by her family's grand estate and, in my opinion, married her with every intention of siphoning off as much as he could get his hands on."

"Roselyn said she kept her money separate throughout their marriage and the house is in her name. Appears he lost out there."

"With Roselyn, yes, as it turns out. But he has his family's wealth to fall back on. He's an only child, so upon the death of his mother, I expect Robby will inherit everything. Sharon can probably obtain the value of their Sacramento estate, but the house alone is worth a couple million."

"Moving on to David. What's his category?"

"Inheritance and investment. David's father was a leading Italian director. Nothing like Fellini famous, but known well enough in Italy. As a youth, David acted in several of his father's films."

"Carson doesn't sound Italian," remarked Ami.

"It's really Caraceni. He opted for the stage name, Carson, when he moved to LA in his mid-twenties. He couldn't adjust to the commercialism of LA filmmaking and moved to New York for the theater. He had some minor roles on Broadway, but never made it big. However, he found freedom and creativity directing small theater productions and made a successful career for himself."

"So, why did he move back to California?"

"Winemaking. David moved to Napa and invested a good bit of his inheritance, and a number of years of sweat, in his friend's small vineyard. It's taken over a decade of hard work and it's a small label, but the wine is excellent and the business is thriving. He's made a good return on his investment."

"So, why'd he leave Napa and move here?"

"Randall had worked with him back east and invited him to direct one of our productions. David liked it here and decided to stay."

"And what about Roger's inheritance?"

"No inheritance. Like us, he works for a living. He's a systems analyst for Beve Technical Solutions in LA. Works remotely. Makes about two hundred thousand a year. Owns a two-bedroom condo at the club and, from what I've heard, his spending tends toward the frugal side."

"Well, it seems since both Robby and David have plenty of money and Roger appears self-sufficient, there would be no financial reason for Justin to call any of them parasites," concluded Ami.

"Not unless they have debts I'm unaware of. I'm sure Sharon can check their financials."

"I'll ask her. Listen, Bill, you can't say a word about any of this. If they find out we're checking on them, it would jeopardize our investigation. Once Lucas makes an arrest, you can gossip all you want, but right now, you need to keep this to yourself. Promise?"

Bill raised his right hand. "I promise."

"Thanks. What do you know about Roselyn?"

"You suspect her, too?"

"No. She offered to help out on the investigation. I value your opinion and wanted your input."

"I'm flattered you think of me that way, mon cher ami." He considered quietly for a moment before answering. "I view Roselyn as intelligent and trustworthy. I can see her as a valuable helper."

"Tell me more about her."

"As I said, she comes from old money so she doesn't flash it around like Robby. She's genuine. Lives her life sensibly. I'd sum her up with a phrase my mother often used, 'she keeps herself above the muck.'"

"Meaning nothing to gossip about?"

"Correct. Of course, there was lots of gossip about Robby's cheating and their divorce, but she stayed clean. Didn't fall into any of the typical pièges du divorce."

"How do you mean?"

"As you know, divorce often diminishes people. It breaks their spirit, hits their insecurities, evokes their anger. They fall to pieces or have affairs or get revenge. Roselyn engaged in none of that. She held her head high, kept her mouth shut and moved on. I admire her for that."

"She admires you, too, especially your gardening skills. She mentioned you gave her gardening club a tour of this beautiful garden."

"I enjoyed that. Roselyn is an excellent gardener in her own right. That hybrid rose of hers took her several tries and it's a show stopper."

"I saw it in her garden and it's beautiful. Bill, I'm curious about something. Why is Roselyn Shelby's only friend? Oh, I realize Shelby can be selfish and, currently, has all this suspicion around her, but surely it wasn't always this way. She's lived here over a year. What happened?"

"This small, gossipy community of ours, for all its faults, is mostly welcoming. Justin was a long-time resident with many friends. When Shelby married and joined him here, we warmly welcomed her. It wasn't long before her behavior started to distance people. She went out of her way to flirt with the men, but made no attempts to befriend the women. And once the rumors started about her affairs, no one, other than Roselyn, remained friendly."

"And, now that she's suspected of killing Justin, she's ostracized."

"Yes, but I think it was her latest disrespectful stunt with Ethan that was the straw. I'd consider her in exile."

>=<

"I was able to uncover a few interesting bits on David, Roger and Robby, but nothing substantial," advised Sharon.

"I'll settle for crumbs at this point."

"None are currently in debt, but David and Robby engage in risky hobbies."

"Then, let's start with Roger so we can set him aside," guided Ami.

"Roger's finances prove negligible. He lives well within his systems analyst salary. No history of debt or gambling. His portfolio is solid and conservative at five hundred thousand," advised Sharon.

"On to David and his risky hobby."

"David likes to gamble."

"You mean like at casinos?"

"No. He enjoys investing in new businesses," explained Sharon.

"Oh, right. Bill said he invested in a Napa winery that's doing great."

"True. Currently, he is heavily subsidizing a marijuana farm outside LA. The management team they hired mishandled the startup. Firing them and starting over has been costly. Without David's continuous backing, they would have gone under."

"But he's not personally going under?"

"His reserves are solid," confirmed Sharon.

"And Robby's risky hobby?"

"Although he is currently solvent, he has a history of debt."

"What caused the debt?"

"He overextends himself with toys."

"Toys?"

"He has a small, but impressive, yacht, a two million dollar sports car and a single-engine plane."

"What? No jet?" mocked Ami. "Wait a minute, this yacht brings up a question for me. Bill said that after Terese threw him out, Robby had to live with Lily while he was closing on his condo. If he has a yacht, why not stay there?"

"The yacht is a fairly recent purchase. Most likely, post Lily."

"Do you think Robby's interest in Lily and Terese had to do with their money? Bill thinks Robby married Roselyn for her money."

"Bill has far more knowledge of the love affairs in this community. However, I would agree that money influences many of Robby's decisions."

"Then it's likely he wanted money from Roselyn, Terese, Lily and maybe Shelby. Did he get any?"

"Per this documentation, Terese, Lily and Shelby provided none. Roselyn granted a few loans during their marriage, then refused to fund him further."

"Did he pay her back?"

"Yes, as a requirement of their divorce settlement."

"So where did he get loans after Roselyn?"

Sharon smiled. "His mommy."

"Spoiled little boy. Nice he had somewhere to go after Roselyn refused to fund him," suggested Ami.

"Perhaps Roselyn was not so much refusing as running low on funds herself. At our lunch, I noticed that emerald ring she was wearing was faux."

"Wait a minute, Roselyn was wearing fake jewelry?"

"I recognized it as a simulation immediately. It was a quality imitation, but definitely not an emerald."

"Hold on, I need clarification. We're on opposite ends of the gem spectrum. You're an expert and I couldn't tell an emerald from green glass, but what about others? Would Arthur, Bill, Shelby, etc., be able to tell it was fake?"

"I doubt any of them would have noticed."

"Let's agree to keep this between us until we know more," suggested Ami. "Wait a minute, maybe Roselyn wore the fake on purpose. Don't rich women often wear copies of their jewelry for safety reasons?"

"Perhaps when traveling, but doubtful in one's own neighborhood," advised Sharon.

"Roselyn being broke doesn't fit her profile. Bill said she's from old money and doesn't flaunt it. Also, her house and gardens are beautifully well-kept. Do you really think Roselyn is broke?"

"I am certain her ring was not an emerald. I have no idea as to her finances. Would you like me to make inquiries?"

"Of course."

>=<

"Hello, Love!   Oh, you're looking pensive," observed Lucas, joining Ami on the deck.

"I think I've hit a dead end."

"Been there," he commiserated. He bent down and kissed her. "I'm beat. Going to get out of this uniform and enjoy a glass of wine. Care for one?"

"Yes, thanks," she replied.

He returned shortly with two glasses and sat next to her. He took a sip of wine before asking, "So, care to talk it over?"

"We've been checking out Shelby's affairs as possible suspects. David, Roger and Robby were at the theater that day, but I can't find a motive for any of them."

"You didn't mention Ethan."

"He wasn't at the theater."

"Are you sure?"

"Lucas, are you saying Ethan was at the theater the day Justin was poisoned?"

"Yes, he was there."

"I can't believe you're providing me with information. I'm happy for it, but it's so unlike you."

"It's hardly police information. You can ask Josh or anyone there that day."

"But I did ask and he's not on the list of cast members," insisted Ami.

"Did you ask for a list of crew?"

Ami stared at him. "I can't believe how stupid I've been. I only asked about the cast."

"You are not stupid. You overlooked a small point. Don't be so hard on yourself."

"So, Ethan was on the crew. Would you be willing to tell me what he does or do I have to call Josh?"

"He volunteers to manage the sound and lighting systems. He wasn't scheduled to be there that day, but they called him in to check out some feedback problems."

"Since you're being free with information, did you recover Justin's missing thermos and was there potassium in it?"

"Yes."

"Wow! Don't know why you're talking, but I love it. Did you happen to find a bottle of potassium?"

"Yep."

"Find any DNA evidence on either?"

He raised his eyebrow.

"Can't blame me for trying. I'm feeling better now that you gave me a lead on Ethan."

"Glad to hear it."

"I can see you're tired so I'll give you some quiet time to watch the ocean. I bought salmon filets and potato salad at the market. I'll take care of the grilling and call you when dinner's ready. You just sit here and relax," said Ami, rising from her chair.

"Thanks, Love. I appreciate that."

Ami bent down and kissed him warmly.

"You're being exceptionally solicitous in exchange for a bit of information," he noted.

"Maybe you should provide it more often."

>=<

"Hi, Ami, it's Sharon. I obtained the financial information on Roselyn."

"Is she in debt?"

"No. Financially secure for years. There have been no large withdrawals or selling off of investments. Her finances are solid."

"Thanks for checking."

"More importantly, I heard from Justin's attorney. It appears Justin purchased an emerald and received some unsettling information when he took it to a jeweler to have it set in a necklace for Shelby."

"I assume we're on the same page about this."

"Yes. The responsible course of action would be to meet with Roselyn," suggested Sharon.

"I agree. Under the circumstances, it might be better if you called her. You could explain it better. Do you mind?"

"Not at all. Are you available all week?"

"Yes."

"I plan to take Clarence along," advised Sharon.

"Good idea. He'll be our insurance. Thanks!"

>=<

"Bill, I need information on Ethan. Tell me all you know about him."

"That's quite a bit. Where would you like to start?"

"Women. Is he married?"

"Divorced."

"Amicably?"

"Oh, yes. He and Kathy were very civil about it."

"Kathy? Not Kathy Riggs?"

"Yes."

"What? Why didn't you mention this before? She has a direct connection to Justin."

"I assumed you knew. It's hardly a secret. Calm yourself, mon cher ami."

"Sorry. I just found out Ethan was at the rehearsal the day Justin died and now I'm finding out he was married

128

to Kathy. No wonder she was livid about Shelby taking him to Justin's service."

"Kathy would have no reason to be jealous of Ethan and Shelby's affair. And Ethan would have no reason to be jealous of Justin and Kathy's friendship. They divorced years ago and there was no animosity between them. Both have had relationships since."

"Jealousy aside, let's focus on a motive for Ethan to have killed Justin."

"I see no motive and his personality doesn't fit. He's a quiet fellow."

Ami stamped her foot. "That's exactly what they say about serial killers."

"Oh, my, you are intense. Calme-toi. I promise to cooperate. What do you want to know about him?"

"What was the reason he and Kathy divorced?"

"They simply grew up and out of the relationship. Often typical of those who marry young."

"Any children?"

"No."

"I understand he does the lighting and sound for the theater. Is that what he does for a living?"

"That's his hobby. His career is physical therapy. And he's a miracle worker. Fixed my back after a garden injury several years ago. Gave me strengthening and stretching exercises that continue to maintain my alignment to this day."

"Good for you. What about affairs before and since his divorce?"

"That didn't sound sincere, but I'll let it slide since you're in a volatile mood. No affairs prior divorce."

"You're sure of that?" challenged Ami.

"Yes. Not a hint or I'd have heard. Post-divorce, he had a long term relationship with Sally Gregson, a nurse at the urgent care. She wanted marriage. He didn't. She took a job in another state and moved."

"When did he start the relationship with Shelby?"

"Last year. Although I'd hardly call their affair a relationship."

"Why not?"

"It was a few hook ups. Physique sans émotion."

"But he escorted her to Justin's celebration of life when she asked him to protect her."

"My understanding is she called and begged a favor. Obliging her would fit with Ethan's personality."

"You're not giving me much to go on here, Bill."

"I'm sorry, mon cher ami. I can't create a villain because you want one."

>=<

"Thanks for fitting me in today. I was so happy you had a cancellation. Bill recommended you highly," flattered Ami.

"I'm pleased to hear it. Now, what problem brings you to see me?" asked Ethan.

"About a week ago, I pulled my shoulder lifting a box of painting supplies out of my trunk. I've been doing yoga stretches to try to work through it, but it continues to bother me. I was hoping you could suggest some helpful exercises for my shoulder, like you did for Bill's back."

"I understand. Let's start by assessing your range of motion."

>=<

"How did your specious appointment with Ethan fare?" inquired Sharon.

"I have to admit, he was pleasant and helpful. Bill doesn't consider him a good candidate. So far, I don't have a motive for him either."

"My knowledge of Ethan is limited to the rare theater interaction. In those, he seemed reputable."

"If he's so reputable, why was he having an affair with a married woman?"

"He can hardly be blamed for responding to Shelby's advances."

"How do you know she made the advances?"

"She admitted it at lunch," reminded Sharon. "I believe her exact words were 'I gave him a kiss that lifted more than his spirits.'"

"She's not shy, is she?"

"One could say the same about you."

>=<

"David and Elise had an animated conversation about you at rehearsals today, Ami," mentioned Josh.

Ami, Lucas and Bill had joined Josh for dinner at Off Broadway.

"Really? What about?"

"He was commenting on her portrait and admiring your talent. Naturally, she raved about you. He plans to call you about commissioning a portrait."

"Don't you find that odd?"

"No. Why should I?" puzzled Josh.

Ami turned to Bill. "Don't you?"

"It doesn't sound odd to me either."

"What's bothering you about it?" asked Lucas.

"The timing. David's in the heat of rehearsals with opening night coming up. He's had a murder right there in the theater that's disrupted his cast. It sounds to me like he'd be focused on the play and not his portrait. Maybe the portrait request is his way of trying to get close to me to find out if I have any evidence that he killed Justin."

"Does he know he's one of your suspects?" asked Lucas.

131

"I hope not."

"I'm sure David has no intention of contacting you until after close of production. I doubt he's even aware of your investigation. He simply saw Elise's portrait on the mantel and decided he wanted one, too. This has nothing to do with Justin's death," asserted Josh.

"As far as I'm concerned, everything everyone does at that theater has to do with Justin's death."

Bill patted Ami's hand. "I'm observing an intensity in you, mon cher ami. First, with the questions about Ethan and now this reaction to David."

"I'm not intense. I'm determined. There's a difference."

"In any case, I never intended to put this kind of pressure on you. Please, stop your investigation. I'm willing to settle for whatever Lucas discovers."

Lucas grinned. "Thanks, Bill, appreciate that vote of confidence."

"My pleasure, mon bon ami."

>=<

"Do you want to talk about what's bothering you?" ventured Lucas, as they sat on the deck enjoying the evening breeze.

"I wish I knew. Bill was right tonight. I'm feeling intense about this."

"You might consider taking a couple days break. I know it's helped me when I get intense about a case."

"So, why do you? Get intense, I mean."

"It usually happens when I'm trying to make the pieces fit instead of allowing them to fit."

"That makes sense. I think that's what I've been trying to do." Ami got up from her chair and put her arms around him. "Thanks for being so supportive. I love you. You really are a wonderful husband."

"I know."

>=<

"Ami said she and Sharon had fun today. What about you Arthur?" asked Lucas.

"I found it very stressful," confessed Arthur. "It's more difficult than you realize trying not to move. I'm not sure how I'll make it through the dress rehearsal and three performances. I'm terrified I'll sneeze and ruin the whole show."

Sharon patted his shoulder. "You are pressuring yourself unduly, Dearest. Of course, you are allowed to move."

"David directed us not to move."

"He directed us to refrain from grand or sudden movements that could pull audience attention away from the main characters," explained Sharon. Just then, her phone buzzed and she glanced at the caller. "Excuse me, I must take this." She rose from her chair and walked away from the table.

"I fear I'll ruin the play. Perhaps, I should drop out."

"Maybe you'd feel less stressed if you just enjoyed the party," suggested Ami.

"I'm not following."

"The scene is real people at a fun party with singing and laughter. Real people move. You can move, just don't throw your arms around or stand up."

"But what if I sneeze or my leg gets a cramp?"

"Try to be subtle about it."

"I'm far too self-conscious about what my body might do. Why aren't you?"

"I guess I was too busy enjoying the show. The lines and the lyrics are clever and funny and the music is

133

upbeat. Never thought about my body. I was too caught up in the show.”

“Why don’t you try that, Arthur?” suggested Lucas. “Focus on enjoying the show.”

“Yes. That sounds a helpful distraction. Thank you.”

“Ami, that was Roselyn,” informed Sharon, returning to the table. “We’re meeting Thursday morning at ten.”

“What was her reaction?”

“Surprised, but appreciative.”

“It’s Justin and Clarence she needs to thank. I hope she confirms our suspicions.”

“I fully expect confirmation.”

“Sharon?” interrupted Arthur. “Am I to assume you’re playing an active part in Ami’s investigation?”

“Yes, I am.”

“Phone inquiries are one thing, but this...this going around questioning people, this is far too dangerous. Someone might harm you.”

“Arthur, we are visiting Roselyn at her beautiful home in the light of day, not meeting hoodlums on a rickety dock at midnight.”

Ami began to laugh.

“Ami, I do not find Sharon’s safety amusing.”

“Sorry, Arthur, but you’re making too much of this. We are perfectly safe. Lucas?” cued Ami.

“Arthur, I assure you, if I felt Ami and Sharon were in danger, I’d have the police escort them.”

“Good idea. I’d feel much better if you did.”

“Lucas, don’t you dare,” warned Ami.

>=<

“I am so grateful to you for bringing this to my attention. My father gave me this ring after my mother

died. She was never much for jewelry. Neither am I, but she always wore this ring in tribute to her family. It was her great-grandmother's. And I wear it in memory of my mother." Roselyn looked down at her hand. "It has, had, great sentimental value." She slipped the ring off her finger and set it on the table.

"Great monetary value as well. The original is a rare Trapiche emerald," advised Clarence.

"Really? How do you know that?" asked Ami.

"I'm familiar with it. Roselyn's father had me resize the ring for Roselyn's slender finger." Clarence turned to Roselyn. "That's why I immediately recognized the emerald as yours when Justin brought it to me."

"Do you really think I'll get it back?"

"Yes, I do. Justin fully intended for the emerald to be returned to you. He had me provide his attorney with an affidavit."

"I'll have my attorney contact his and hopefully negotiate the return," stated Roselyn.

"They can call on me to assist in those efforts. And once the legalities are resolved, I would like to reset it for you with my compliments."

"Thank you. You've been more than kind."

"I'm assuming Justin had no idea Robby had stolen the emerald from Roselyn," said Ami.

"None. Robby told him it was stock closeout from his business. Justin had no idea of the emerald's real value. He brought it to me and asked me to make a pendant as a birthday gift for Shelby. He was shocked and saddened when I relayed my suspicions."

"Robby knew how much my mother's ring meant to me. I feel heartbroken that he'd rob me of a treasured heirloom and sell it like it meant nothing."

Clarence picked up the ring off the table and turned it in his hand. "This is a quality imitation, but the color is

much brighter than the original. It's curious Robby didn't choose a closer color match."

"Maybe he didn't have one in his closeout stock," shot Ami.

"I noticed the lighter color, too, and asked him about it. He said it was due to the cleaning removing years of build up. It's an old ring, it sounded reasonable, so I accepted his explanation. I never, ever, imagined he'd steal from me."

"So, that was how he stole it," said Ami. "He offered to clean it for you?"

"No, the bezel cracked and the stone came loose. Robby took the ring to repair it. I guess he thought it was a perfect opportunity to steal it."

"A bezel setting is most secure. Would Robby have had any opportunity to cut it?" asked Clarence.

"I took it off every night and placed it on the dresser."

"I suspect that's when he did it," offered Ami. "I'm wondering if all of Robby's closeout stock was stolen. Clarence, were you ever asked to reset other stones he'd sold?"

"A few, but this was the first gem I recognized and had reason to question."

"Perhaps Clarence would be willing to examine all of your jewelry," suggested Sharon.

"I'd be happy to," agreed Clarence.

"I'd appreciate that."

"You realize what we've verified, don't you? This confirms the incident Kathy was talking about," said Ami. "Robby is the person Justin confronted before he died. The theft of the emerald is Robby's motive for killing Justin."

"After what Robby did to me, I don't want to defend him, but I can't believe he could kill anyone," disputed Roselyn.

"I can understand it's hard for you to believe something so terrible about him. But think about it. He's cheated. He's stolen. You didn't believe he'd do those things either. It's possible he could have done this, too."

"Yes, I suppose it's possible. I feel like we're talking about some criminal I've never met. This is a person I was married to."

"Well, when you confront Robby about the ring, don't mention he's a suspect in Justin's murder. We don't want him to know we're on to him," advised Ami.

"I may not confront him personally. I'm worried I won't be able to restrain myself. I have this overwhelming urge to sock him in the eye."

"Don't do it. He'll charge you with assault."

"I won't, but I'm not letting him get away with this. When I talk to my attorney about the return of the emerald, I'm asking him to report the theft to the police. I want to see Robby arrested and jailed."

>=<

Sharon straightened her shoulders as Robby was escorted into her living room. "Robby, this is a surprise."

"I received a call from Roselyn. She was upset. She said you and Ami instigated some issue about her jewelry."

"Correction. I believe it was you who instigated the jewelry issue."

"This was a private matter between me and Roselyn. It was none of your business!"

"You may not raise your voice to me," reproached Sharon.

"I have every right to be angry. Because of your meddling, the police are now involved. You're trying to destroy my reputation."

"If your reputation is destroyed, that is your doing, not mine."

"You started this. You had no right to interfere!"

"What is all this shouting?" complained Arthur, joining them from the garden. He was dressed for golf and carrying his putter. "It's disturbing my practice."

"Robby came to confront me about speaking with Roselyn," calmly informed Sharon.

"Confront you? How dare you shout at Sharon. You are to leave this house at once. Out! Out I say!" ordered Arthur, raising his putter.

"May I be of assistance?" asked Sharon's house manager, quietly entering the room. He was a large, imposing man.

"Please escort Mr. Kelly out, Thomas," directed Sharon.

"My pleasure," he replied, taking a step toward Robby.

"You'll pay for this, Sharon. You and Ami," warned Robby, brushing past Thomas. He exited the room with Thomas closely behind.

Sharon smiled at Arthur. "Thank you for so bravely defending me, Dearest."

"It was my pleasure and my duty. Now, we must address this threat. I'm calling Lucas at once."

>=<

"Ami, it's Robby Kelly calling. Roselyn showed me that excellent portrait you painted of her and I'd like to commission you to paint mine."

"I'm sure we can arrange that."

"Wonderful! I was hoping you could join me on my yacht tomorrow to discuss it."

"Your yacht? Oh, I assume that's the background you want for your portrait."

"Yes, I want myself painted on deck in my yachting cap. Is that a problem?"

"As a background, no. But I'm afraid my time is committed until after the play. I would think yours would be, too. You're in the ensemble, aren't you?"

"Yes. I didn't intend for us to start the painting right away. I'm proposing a preliminary meeting to discuss it."

"I'm sorry, Robby, but I won't be able to meet with you until we're finished with the play. I hope that's okay?"

"Certainly. Let's discuss it then. Goodbye."

>=<

"Had a few interesting calls and visits today," said Lucas, relaxing with Ami on the deck before dinner.

"Was one of them from Arthur?"

"Yes. I assume Sharon informed you."

"She called me while he was calling you. Seems Robby is unhappy about our meeting with Roselyn. Robby contacted me today, too, but by phone."

"And said?"

"I'll fill you later. Right now, I want to focus on Roselyn. When she called me today, she said her attorney helped her file a theft complaint against Robby. Was that one of your visits?"

"Yes. Any background you'd like to provide?"

"It all started when Shelby and Roselyn joined Sharon and me for lunch. Sharon noticed that the emerald ring Roselyn had on was fake. Then, Justin's attorney told Sharon that he had an affidavit about an emerald Justin had bought from Robby. It seems when Justin took it to Clarence to set in a necklace for Shelby's birthday, Clarence recognized it as the rare gem he had resized for Roselyn's father. When Clarence told Justin of his suspicions, Justin had him write an affidavit for his attorney. So, we took Clarence with us to meet with Roselyn. He confirmed the gem in Roselyn's ring as a fake and examined Roselyn's other jewelry and discovered several more fake pieces. Robby stole the real gems and replaced them with fakes."

"Stop and breathe," ordered Lucas.

Ami took a deep breath.

"Roselyn's attorney provided other documentation regarding gems not belonging to Roselyn. Any idea how he got those records?"

"Clarence may have helped him obtain private sales affidavits. Other customers had brought Clarence gems they'd bought from Robby, too. But Roselyn's emerald was the first one that raised his suspicions. It seems Robby was selling people the stolen gems, telling them it was closeout stock leftover from his jewelry business."

"No wonder Robby was miffed at the two of you. You uncovered his scam."

"Sharon described him as being a lot more than miffed. She said he threatened us when he was leaving."

"It's in her statement," noted Lucas.

"The most important part of all this is we uncovered more than Robby's scam. We know now why Justin confronted someone and we know that confrontation was with Robby. Robby is our killer."

"If true, he's a suspect," clarified Lucas.

"Our number one suspect," emphasized Ami.

"I think now that you've made this discovery, you and Sharon should take a break. Let me handle this."

"You mean because Robby threatened us?"

"That's one reason. The other is my case is coming to a tipping point. If you keep asking questions, I'm worried you'll inadvertently walk into danger or tip someone off. It's too risky now."

"I love that you want to protect me, but I want to see this through."

"Seriously, I'm asking you to put your investigation on pause until the play is over."

"You mean because we'll be in the theater with Robby and he might try to poison us, too?"

"Please, Love. Put my mind at ease. I don't want to have to worry about you."

"I don't want you to worry either. It might distract you and that could put you in danger. Okay, I agree to pause until the play is over."

"Thank you." Lucas leaned over and kissed her.

"Arthur will be happy. He's been upset with me for involving Sharon. He's worried she'll get killed. Sharon said he bravely defended her today, although I doubt someone as robust as Robby was afraid of a seventy-six year old with a golf club."

"Arthur does have a solid swing."

"Well, unlike his threat to Sharon, Robby was very cordial to me. Said he had seen Roselyn's portrait and wanted his painted."

"Interesting timing."

"Yes. And it was a deliberate lie. I specifically asked Roselyn about it when she called today and she said he's never seen her portrait. He pretended to act like he and Roselyn had a friendly discussion so I wouldn't be suspicious of him. And get this, he wanted me to join him on the deck of his yacht to discuss his portrait. I envisioned him sailing us out to sea, water all around, no witnesses."

"So, you declined."

"Of course."

"Good. It's such an ordeal recovering bodies lost at sea."

"Assuming mine?"

"I was thinking his. You're a dangerous competitor when riled."

Ami smiled.

CHAPTER TEN

The Dress

"All right, everyone, we're about to begin our final dress. We expect full speed," announced David Carson. "Ensemble, you're a little thin. Robust voices, please. However, no straining. We need all of you to remain healthy."

All of the singers nodded their understanding.

"Extras, please watch your stance. No pulling focus." He nodded to them.

Arthur, Sharon and Ami along with Roselyn, who had been asked last minute to fill out the seating, nodded back from the sofas and chairs upstage.

"Bill has agreed to be our outside eye and will provide notes to Randall," continued David.

"Set, Bill?"

"Set!" called Bill from the audience.

"Ethan, set with tech elements?" asked David.

"All set," called Ethan from the soundboard.

"Randall and Josh will focus on pace. Ready, Randall?"

"Ready!" called Randall from the audience.

"Leo? Orchestra set?"

"Set!" called the conductor from the pit."

"Set, Josh?"

"Set," answered Josh from his piano, stage left.

"When you're ready," directed David to Elise and Malcolm.

>=<

"DNA results are conclusive. It's touch DNA so good chance it will get disputed, but we can back it up with the other documentation," stated Investigation Bureau

Commander Johnson. "What do you say? Ready to go to the DA for a warrant?"

"Yes, we have more than enough," replied Lucas.

>=<

"Well done, everyone," praised David. "As you know, Sharon is hosting a socializing for us at the club tonight."

"Yoo-hoo!" cheered several of the group.

"Eight sharp. I expect everyone on time as a sign of respect to Sharon."

"Free food and booze. You can expect us early," called out one of the group. The rest laughed.

"I want you to enjoy each other's company tonight, and while you're enjoying, I'd like you to remember that you've been given a full day and night off between this final and opening night to rest, not nurse a hangover, so please watch your alcohol intake," cautioned David.

Several chuckled.

"I'm serious. Our audience expects and deserves us to be energized on opening night. Agreed?"

Everyone nodded agreement.

As the cast and crew began to file out, David approached the extras. "May I have a quick word, Roselyn?" he asked, escorting her away from the group.

Ami turned to Bill. "What's that about?"

"I noticed Roselyn angrily staring over at Robby a number of times. It pulled my focus. Randall noticed as well and put it in his notes. David is addressing it with her privately."

"Is that really necessary?" questioned Arthur.

"No need to be overprotective. He'll be gentle with her," assured Bill.

"I suppose it's understandable she would feel resentment toward Robby after what he did to her," observed Arthur.

"No, I don't think it's about the divorce," countered Bill. "This anger was ripe. I think it's about something going on right now."

Arthur opened his mouth to speak and Sharon nudged him. He shut it and remained silent.

Ami and Sharon exchanged glances.

"You all know something!" accused Bill. "What? Out with it."

"I'm sorry, Bill, we can't discuss it," answered Ami.

His eyes penetrated Sharon's.

"No comment," she stated.

"Arthur?"

Arthur lowered his head and remained silent.

"You're infuriating!" charged Bill, stomping away.

>=<

"I wanted to apologize before you left. It was me and Randall who noted your anger at Robby. Are you okay?"

"Of course, Bill. No need to apologize. You were right to note it. David was very kind. I promised him it wouldn't happen again. I don't want my anger ruining the performance."

"Do you mind if I ask why you were so angry with Robby? You know how inquisitive I am. I won't rest until I know," confessed Bill.

Roselyn laughed. "Bill, you are nothing if not honest about yourself. Okay," she nodded, "I'll not only tell you, I'll give you permission to gossip about it all you like."

"Oh, goody!" Bill smiled broadly.

"Robby stole my family's jewels and sold them."

The smile vanished from Bill's face. "I'm so sorry, Roselyn. I truly am." He reached for her hand and patted it gently. "Losing your cherished family gems must hurt you deeply. They represent memories and history. No wonder you were so angry."

"Thank you for understanding the important point in all this."

"What are you going to do about it?"

"Hopefully, see him arrested."

>=<

"It's nearly eight. Shouldn't they be here by now?" asked Arthur.

"I expect everyone to arrive on time," soothed Sharon.

"I'm looking forward to tonight. After all these months of work and stress, it will be good for us to let loose and relax together," said Josh.

"David seemed pleased with rehearsal today," commented Ami. "And, Arthur, you were more relaxed."

"Yes, I admit I wasn't nearly as self-conscious. Thanks for the tip about focusing on the play. It was a helpful distraction."

"Hello, everyone," greeted Lucas, joining them. He put his arm around Ami and gave her a quick kiss.

"Did you notice any of the cast in the parking lot?" asked Arthur.

"Yes. Several of them were pulling in."

"Good. I'm happy they're on time," said Josh. "David intends to get everyone out of here by midnight."

>=<

"Tonight's gathering is about relaxing, enjoying one another's company and extending friendship," announced Sharon. "To friendship!"

"To friendship!" cheered the cast and crew.

Roselyn got up from the table and walked over to Robby. "What you did was unforgiveable. I hope to see you in jail," she said, tossing the champagne from her glass in his face. She set the glass on the table, turned her back to him and proceeded out the door.

The room went silent.

Robby sat, open-mouthed for a moment, before picking up his napkin, wiping his face, rising from his chair and leaving the room.

The room began to buzz.

Meg nudged Ami. "Honey, he must have done something wicked to get Roselyn that pissed."

Bill raised his head to Ami and Sharon and nodded knowingly.

>=<

Making good on his direction for the cast and crew to rest, David scooted out the last of the group by midnight.

Ami, Lucas, Bill, Josh, Sharon and Arthur remained behind, after the guests had departed, to gossip.

"Okay, let's address the elephant," began Bill. "Roselyn's theatrics surprised me. Very unlike her. She's usually so proper."

"Totally out of character for her," agreed Josh.

"I think Robby handled it well by following her lead and leaving immediately," noted Arthur. "It would have been uncomfortable for everyone had either of them stayed."

"You mean out of sight, out of mind?" suggested Ami.

"Exactly," confirmed Arthur.

"Well, it wasn't out of my mind," said Bill. "And I know why she did it."

Ami stared at him. "Do you?"

"Yes. I spoke with Roselyn this afternoon. She told me Robby took her family gems and sold them."

"He's a cad!" condemned Arthur. "You do not rob a woman of her heirlooms."

"I'm surprised she told you. I would have thought she'd want to keep it confidential," said Ami.

"Not only did she tell me, she gave me permission to pass it on. It appears she wants Robby's reputation destroyed."

"Deservedly," agreed Arthur.

"Did Roselyn tell you Justin confronted Robby about it?"

"No." Bill's face became stoic. "You're referring to your theory. Does this mean Robby killed Justin?"

"No, Bill," quickly interjected Lucas. "Robby is one of many suspects."

Ami turned to Lucas with surprise. "Many?"

"Yes," Lucas answered with a silencing stare.

>=<

"Wow! That sky is so clear I feel I can reach up and pluck the stars down," envisioned Lucas, as he and Ami cuddled on the deck chaise lounge before bed.

"The stars can wait. I need to know more about these many suspects."

"Can I assume you're not going to let us enjoy this moment until I do?"

"Yes, you can. I thought we agreed that Robby was the killer."

"I never agreed to that."

"Yes, you did. We were talking about Robby confronting Sharon and threatening us when you said your case was coming to a tipping point and you wanted me to pause my investigation so I'd be safe. You gave me the impression you were ready to arrest Robby for Justin's murder."

"If I gave you that impression, I apologize. That was not my intention."

"So, what you told Bill is true then? You consider Robby one of many suspects?"

"Yes."

"I'm not happy about this," stated Ami.

"I can see that."

>=<

"I thought this needed to be addressed, Ami," suggested Sharon.

"Is there any indication that Justin knew about this?"

"Since he had not advised his attorney or questioned Clarence, I would assume not."

"We need to speak with Shelby and Roselyn."

"I believe you made a promise to Lucas regarding pausing our investigation," reminded Sharon.

"I did but that was about moving forward. This is part of what we've already investigated. It doesn't renege on my promise."

"I doubt Lucas would agree."

"He'll understand. Look, if it bothers you, don't come with me. I can fill you in later."

"I fully intend to be present. I made no promise to Lucas."

>=<

"Shelby, why didn't you tell us about buying the aquamarine from Robby?' asked Ami.

148

"Why should I? What I buy is none of your business."

"We think the stolen gems are why Justin confronted Robby, so it could be tied to his murder," emphasized Ami.

"How would I know that?"

"You were aware that we were examining the four men with whom you had affairs. I would have expected you to disclose everything pertaining to those men," counseled Sharon.

"I'm sorry. I didn't know it was important," apologized Shelby, presenting Sharon with a contrite pout.

Ami was amused by the direct contrast between Shelby's responses to her and to Sharon.

"That was from my grandmother's pendant, Shelby. It was a family heirloom," accused Roselyn.

"I had no way of knowing it was yours. It was my favorite color and I thought it'd make a beautiful ring. You can't blame me for buying something I liked."

"Maybe not, but you do understand I want it back. I'll reimburse you what you paid, of course."

"I don't have it anymore. The police took it." She turned to Ami. "Lucas already asked me all about this. You and your husband really need to communicate better."

"Don't deflect," confronted Roselyn. "I'm assuming the police took it as part of my theft complaint."

"If there's a trial, it may be awhile before it's returned to you," noted Ami.

"I can wait. It's never been about wearing the jewelry. I treasured its sentimental value. Having it stolen is like losing my family members all over again. I feel incredibly hurt."

"I'm sorry my buying it hurt you," apologized Shelby, "but it's not my fault! Anyway, the police will give it back to you and they'll make Robby pay me back. So, you won't be losing anything."

"That's hardly the point, Shelby," replied Roselyn.

"I'm relieved you'll get two of the pieces back, Roselyn. Let's hope we can recover them all for you," offered Ami.

"Yes, I'm hopeful, too. I appreciate everything you and Sharon have done to help recover them."

"You're welcome, but it was really Justin and Clarence that uncovered this crime," credited Ami.

"I know. I'm grateful for their integrity."

>=<

"Clarence called me today with a bit of information I think will interest you," teased Sharon.

"Oh?"

"It appears Roger purchased a three carat diamond from Robby several months ago."

"Really? Extravagant purchase for a frugal guy."

"Perhaps Robby offered a discount?" suggested Sharon.

"Sounds like Robby was selling his 'overstock' to everyone at the theater,"

"This morning, Roger presented the diamond to Clarence to design an engagement ring."

"I assume Clarence informed Roger of Robby's stolen stock and referred the matter to the police."

"He handled the situation most tactfully."

"Guess Elise was right about Roger and Sally being in love. Sounds like the relationship is moving forward."

"Although not with that diamond. It was one of Roselyn's gems."

"Hopefully, they'll keep bringing them to Clarence and she'll end up getting them all back. Let's see, so far, he's found the emerald, aquamarine and now a diamond."

"Of the three, the emerald is by far the most valuable. It is a unique and rare gem. I am relieved that was recovered."

"So how many more pieces of her jewelry are still out there?"

"Two. Both important gems. One is a highly polished Mexican turquoise with a TQI of ninety-two that belonged to her three times great grandmother."

"You lost me with TQI," halted Ami.

"It is a standard of measure. The important point to note is only one percent of these stones rate above ninety."

"So it would be old and rare."

"Yes. The other is a twelve carat Extremadura Spanish rose quartz that belonged to her four times great grandmother."

"How do you know all this about her jewelry?"

"Her family had documented assessments on all of the gems," informed Sharon.

"When she talked about heirlooms, I had no idea she meant stuff from four times great grandmothers. Her jewelry has a lot of family history."

"In addition to the history, these are unique gems."

"Well, I wish they all get recovered and returned to her."

"As do I. I further wish she would wear them. The purpose of possessing beautiful gems is to allow others to enjoy them as well."

>=<

"Since you're sad about your jewelry, I thought of something that might cheer you up. Let's take a single's cruise. My treat!" offered Shelby.

"A single's cruise? This is hardly the time for us to take a trip," advised Roselyn.

"Give me one good reason."

151

"I can give you two. Your husband's murder investigation and my theft investigation."

"But the police are handling those. Besides, they don't have anything to do with us," dismissed Shelby.

"I think the police would think differently. They'd expect us to be here in case they have questions."

"I've answered enough of their questions. I don't have anything else to tell them," Shelby whined. "I want to get away and have some fun."

"I'm sure we can find something fun to do around here."

"No, we can't. People are always watching and judging me. They expect me to act like a grieving widow. I want to feel happy and enjoy my life."

Roselyn reached out and touched Shelby's arm. "Shelby, don't you feel sad about Justin being killed?"

"Sure, but I'm not going to fake cry about it," replied Shelby, moving her arm away.

"That doesn't sound sad."

"Well, it's not like we had a future together. He was going to divorce me. Dead or divorced, the marriage was over."

"You realize your viewpoint is particularly self-serving."

"Of course!"

"That wasn't a compliment, Shelby."

>=<

"Lucas, I need an answer. Are you going to arrest Robby or not?"

"Yes, for theft."

"Of Roselyn's jewelry," finished Ami.

"Her gems are part of it."

"I knew he stole other people's stuff, too," triumphed Ami. "I told Sharon I'd bet money it was more than just Roselyn's. Please tell me you're eventually going to arrest him for Justin's murder."

"You might not want to bet on that one."

>=<

"Well, Robby's definitely out of the picture. Lucas is not arresting him for Justin's murder."

"Which means?" inquired Sharon.

"We're back to Shelby, David, Ethan and Roger," sighed Ami.

"I thought we exonerated each of them."

"Obviously, too soon. It's all my fault. I let the theft of the jewelry limit my focus to Robby. I'm sorry."

"No need to apologize."

"No more pauses. Investigation is back on."

"Lucas will not be happy with you."

"Too bad. He misled me."

"I fear this may become your first marital disagreement."

"Well, there was bound to be one sooner or later."

Sharon smiled.

"Other than Shelby, money seems to be out as a motive. And I don't think she has the discipline to plan, research, follow through and remove evidence."

"I concur," said Sharon.

"I think we should revisit Ethan. Why would he escort Shelby to Justin's service? That irks me."

"Both Bill and Roselyn suggested it was chivalry," reminded Sharon.

"Maybe, but I think he's got feelings for her. He was at the theater that day. He didn't know Justin planned the divorce. He could have poisoned Justin in order to have Shelby. Let's keep him on our active list. And we might as well put Roger there, too. Kathy hurt him when she

153

dropped him for Justin. He could have killed Justin so he could win her back.”

“Is it a viable motive considering his relationship with Sally Kirby and his purchase of the diamond for an engagement ring?”

“Probably not, but, like the others, he was at the theater the day Justin was poisoned and how do we know the ring was for Sally? Maybe he planned to propose to Kathy? As for David, I’ve got no motive, nothing. Oh, I wish we had some clear evidence against someone.”

A soft smile framed Sharon’s lips.

“What?”

“Your intensity and interest in continuing this investigation amuses me.”

“Why?”

“I hardly think I need to explain this, Ami.”

“I think you do, because I don’t get your point.”

“Very well. It is obvious to me, as I am sure it is to you, that Lucas knows who killed Justin and is preparing to make his arrest. Our work is done.”

“How can it be done if we don’t know who killed Justin?” objected Ami.

“We will know when Lucas makes his arrest.”

“I want to know myself. That’s been the whole goal of our investigation.”

“I dispute that. Our investigative goal has been to assist in adjunctive and supportive information gathering. We were to be of benefit to the police, specifically Lucas.”

“And find out who killed Justin,” restated Ami.

“Not so. We were to assist with information gathering, not interfere in the police investigation.”

“Trying to uncover the killer on my own does not interfere with the police.”

“I disagree. We have our purpose. They have theirs. May I present a case in point?”

“Be my guest.”

"The goal of the Theater Guild is to provide financial assistance for the children's hospital. We do not attempt to perform the medical procedures."

Ami looked up sharply, then nodded. "You're right. Point taken."

"And your understanding of it is?" pressed Sharon.

"Wow! When you make a point, you use a laser. Our goal is to assist the police by gathering information, not to try to solve the case to feed my ego. I'm sorry I lost my focus."

"Apology accepted. May I assume we are now refocused on our initial worthy goal?"

"You may."

"May I assume our investigation has ended?"

"No, you may not."

Sharon frowned at her.

"I'm not suggesting we move forward with questioning people. I just want us to keep our eyes and ears open to anything that might present itself. We might still uncover something that could be of benefit to the police."

"Very well," agreed Sharon.

CHAPTER ELEVEN

The Performance

"Attention, everyone, a few reminders," called David Carson. The cast and crew were gathered backstage in a circle. "Right now, you're full of adrenaline which leads to fast delivery. So, aim for a delivery slower than in rehearsals. Remember to breathe. We don't want you passing out on stage."

A few chuckles circulated throughout the group.

"Let's all take a few deep breaths together to focus ourselves."

He led the group in a few deep breaths.

"Good," he approved. "We should expect the unexpected, like someone laughing loudly at a line not meant to be funny or a noisy sneeze in the front row just as you're about to reach that high note."

A few of the actors chuckled, others groaned.

"Let it happen and stay in character."

The group murmured they would.

"I expect each of you to tamp down your ego," continued David. "It's not about individual sparkle. When we work together, everyone shines."

All of the cast nodded in agreement.

"I know you're well prepared and ready to triumph. Just remember, no production is perfect. Accept that something will go wrong. When it happens, no need to panic. Just keep on going and the audience will never know you forget a line or a prop was out of place. It's all new to them. Got it?"

"Got it!" replied the group.

"Finally, let yourselves have fun. If you're enjoying yourselves, the audience will, too. They want to see you do well. They're rooting for you. I know I am. Break a leg." He raised his arm in the air. "Places!"

>=<

After the performance, the cast and crew were huddled in groups backstage, drinking champagne, congratulating one another and chatting with delight and relief.

"Great job everyone! I'm proud of each of you!" called out David to the group.

"We did it!" said Randall, patting Josh on the back. "The audience liked the show."

"Liked? They loved it!" corrected Bill, handing Josh and Randall each a glass of champagne. "Four curtain calls and they laughed and applauded all through it. I expect rave reviews in the morning press."

Josh took a long drink from his glass. "I'm so relieved. The opening went smoother than I imagined. We had a couple of pace flaws, but they recovered swiftly."

"No one noticed," assured Bill.

"I'm still flying high with adrenaline," admitted Josh.

"Drink up," said Randall, raising his glass.

"Attention, everyone," shouted David. "Sharon would like to address us."

"Tonight went beautifully!" complimented Sharon. "Every aspect of the production was professionally and smoothly conducted. Most importantly, the proceeds will be of great benefit to the children's hospital. It is my pleasure to thank you with an opening night remembrance."

Arthur stepped forward with a box and opened it.

Sharon put her hand inside and took out a small wrapped package and handed it to David, shaking his hand. She continued presenting the small packages and shaking hands with each of the cast and crew until all had been served.

"Please, open them!" she encouraged.

Each unwrapping revealed a small gold pin with the name of the musical, *Belt Out*, engraved upon it.

"This is perfect!" announced David. "Thank you, Sharon, from all of us."

Ami nudged Josh and whispered, "Is this a normal opening night thing? I wasn't expecting champagne and gifts."

"Sharon always makes a point of providing the opening night champagne buffet and gifts. The cast and crew have come to look forward to them. Each season the gifts are a little different. This pin is a perfect keepsake. It's beautifully engraved."

"And in keeping with Sharon's good taste, it's twenty-four carat gold," said Bill.

Ami laughed. "Only you would make a point of turning it over to check."

"I bet half the room's done it," informed Bill.

"He's not exaggerating," agreed Josh.

"Hi, Ami!"

"Kathy! I noticed you on stage. I was surprised to see you back so soon. I'm happy you're feeling better."

"Going home helped. And I felt I needed to come back to finish the show. I called and asked if I could rejoin the cast. I was relieved when David, Randall and Josh okayed it."

"Of course, we okayed it. We were thrilled to have you back. You're a valued part of our company," said Josh.

"Thanks. I appreciate that. Well, I just wanted to come say 'Hi!'. Roger's waiting. We're meeting some old friends at his place."

Kathy smiled and walked across the room to where Roger was standing. He put his arm around her and she nuzzled her head into his chest.

"What's going on there?" Ami whispered to Bill.

"Love renewed," he whispered back.

"And Sally?"

"Moved on to David," informed Bill.

"Really? But Elise said Sally and Roger were in love. And Roger asked Clarence to make a diamond ring."

"Appears not to be."

"I thought David was a confirmed bachelor."

"He still is. He and Sally aren't serious."

"Are these relationship changes a typical theater thing?"

"L'amour est capricieux."

"What fickle love are you two whispering about?" asked Josh.

"Nothing. Just idle chatter," dismissed Bill.

"Sounds more like intense gossip," accused Josh.

"Of no importance. Our focus is your successful opening night," cheered Bill.

Josh smiled.

"I'm so happy it was a success. That makes the rest of the shows less stressful for everyone," offered Ami.

"Having a good opening is definitely a boost, but we'll still be anxious," advised Josh.

"Theater people know better than to get cocky," said Randall.

A small group standing nearby laughed and nodded.

Ethan walked up to Randall. "I'll be here early tomorrow to reset the computer."

"Is everything okay?" questioned Randall with concern.

"Just a maintenance double check. All's well."

"Good to hear. Smooth run tonight, man. The sound, the lighting, every cue on time. Great job!" congratulated Randall.

"Thanks," said Ethan. He glanced over toward the opening side door and nodded.

Ami noticed Shelby standing in the doorway waving to him.

"I'm off then," bid Ethan.

"Drive safely," cautioned Randall.

"You bet!" he replied.

Ami watched closely as Ethan walked out the door. She saw Shelby fling her arms around him and hold him in a romantic embrace. Then, the door swung closed.

Ami nudged Bill. "Are they dating?" she whispered.

"Interesting question. Seems this week, they've fallen madly in love."

"You sure it just happened this week?"

"That's the interesting question," replied Bill.

>=<

"So, how did you like the show?" greeted Ami, arriving home.

"It was thoroughly entertaining," replied Lucas. "By the way, you looked right at home up there on stage. Did you have fun at the party?"

"Yes." She gave him a kiss hello. "I'm sorry you weren't allowed to come. Elise said that cast and crew only rule is some kind of tradition." She sat down beside him and slipped off her heels.

"I assume everyone was celebrating the success."

"Bubbling over with joy. David, Randall and Josh were relieved. Everyone worked so hard. I'm glad it went well for them."

"Not just them. You're part of the cast, too."

"Hardly. I just watched the show from the stage instead of the audience."

"I heard Sharon's gift was a hit."

"Oh, let me show you." Ami reached over for her purse. She pulled out the box and handed it to him.

"You have a nice souvenir here," he said, checking out the pin.

"How did you hear about it anyway?"

160

"Bill, of course."

"That was fast! What did he do? Call you from the theater?"

Lucas laughed. "His car."

"I found out some relationship news regarding the cast and crew that might aid your police investigation."

"What's that?"

"Kathy and Roger are back together. Sally has moved on to David. Ethan and Shelby are madly in love."

"And how did you obtain this information?"

"I saw them myself. And Bill filled in the details."

"Okay, thanks," replied Lucas.

"What do you mean 'okay'? This raises questions. Why are people madly in love as soon as Justin is dead? Have they been in love all along? Did Ethan and Shelby conspire to kill Justin so they could be together? Did Roger kill Justin to get Kathy back? Did David…well, I'm still working on him. These relationship changes affect their motives. I'm going to check this out."

"I thought we agreed your investigation was on pause until the end of the show?"

"I'm just going to follow up on these relationships."

"Please don't question anyone in the cast or crew until after closing night."

"Why?"

"Because I'm worried you'll tip someone off. They could run, or, worse, they could hurt you or someone else," warned Lucas.

"This arrest you're about to make, do you have DNA?"

"Yes."

"Good job."

"Glad you approve."

"I assume you won't tell me who you're arresting."

Lucas raised an eyebrow.

"Fine. I promise not to question any of them, but I plan to figure it out before you make your arrest."

>=<

"I think I feel more anxious tonight than I did opening night," confessed Arthur, as they stood backstage waiting for David to gather them.

"You're not alone. I heard some of the cast talking about it, too. It has to do with the fear of not performing as well as the last show," related Roselyn.

"I suppose that makes sense. It does not relieve my anxiety, however."

"It'll be fine, Arthur. Just focus on the show, like you did for the other performances," reassured Ami. "It worked then and it'll work tonight."

"Right."

Ami turned from Arthur to Roselyn. "I notice you seem to have resolved your anger at Robby."

"Taking action helps me cope. Calling my attorney, filing a theft report, even throwing a glass of champagne." Roselyn chuckled softly.

"You totally surprised everyone that night."

"Surprised myself, too. But my anger made me want to hurt him."

"Better champagne than a bullet," supposed Ami.

"All right, everyone, gather round," called David Carson. Ami, Arthur and Roselyn joined the cast and crew forming a circle around him. "Tonight, as you enjoy your closing performance, allow yourself to be in the moment. Revel in this opportunity to join your individual talents in collaboration. Tomorrow, your performances in this exceptional musical will be fond memories. But, tonight, they are still living moments. Come alive in them. Allow yourself to enjoy every minute. Break a leg." He raised his arm in the air. "Places!"

>=<

"It is my pleasure to host you this evening," said Sharon. She had arranged a private room at the club for the closing performance after-party. "I wish to congratulate you on your successful production. You thrilled our audiences. Your performances generously contributed to the children's hospital. Thank you. To you!" Sharon raised her glass to the group.

As Sharon sat down, David stood to speak.

"This was one of our best productions to date. Each of you performed brilliantly and came together as a cohesive company. I thoroughly enjoyed working with you. Please accept my gift to you as a remembrance of this beautiful experience."

He walked around the table, shaking the hands of the cast and crew and presenting each with a ten-inch digital photo frame loaded with rehearsal and performance photos. When he returned to his place at the table, everyone applauded. He raised his glass, "Let's party!"

Music began to play. Some in the group began to dance. Some visited the buffet table.

Ami turned to Roselyn. "I see Shelby and Ethan are together. Bill said they're in love. Is that true?"

"For the moment, yes. How long before she's bored with him is anyone's guess."

"So, turns out it wasn't an affair. They've been in love all along."

"Just the opposite. It was a meaningless affair that is suddenly heartfelt love. Shelby's gushing about the thrill of new love. I'm afraid she's pretending. To his credit, Ethan seems to be well aware that the odds of this lasting are poor."

"What do you mean pretending? She doesn't love him?"

"I could be wrong, but ever since Shelby told us about her young affair with Jon Abel, I can't help but think she's been trying to recreate the love she felt for him. She can't, of course, so all her relationships turn out to be pretend," analyzed Roselyn.

"And pretend love eventually ends in disappointment, like it did with Justin."

"Yes," agreed Roselyn.

Bill joined them at the table. "What are you two gossiping about?"

Ami nodded toward Ethan and Shelby.

"Vrai amour ou faux amour?"

"Well, Bill, whether it's true or fake, they seem happy tonight."

"I agree."

Will Lawson walked up to their table. "Hi, everyone," he greeted.

"Please join us, Will," invited Bill.

"I just came over to ask Roselyn if she'd care to dance."

"I'd love to," she replied.

As Roselyn and Will joined the others on the dance floor, Bill leaned into Ami and lowered his voice. "As for our other couple, it appears Roger and Kathy can't keep their hands off one another. They've been physically attached since they arrived."

"I noticed them kissing. Now it looks like they're leaving."

"Sexe passionné. That's my guess for why they're heading home early."

"They have all night for sex. You'd think they could postpone it a little while longer. The party just started. It seems rude to leave so soon."

"Spoken like a old married woman. Where's your hubby tonight? Why isn't he here?"

"I thought this was cast and crew only, like on opening night, and told him he wasn't invited. Now I wish he was here to dance with me."

"It would be my pleasure, mon cher ami. Come, let me delight you with my smooth moves."

CHAPTER TWELVE

The Arrest

"How was the closing night party?" greeted Lucas as he entered the house.

"Great. Turns out it wasn't restricted. You could have come after all."

"Just as well. I was busy." He gave her a kiss and sat down beside her.

Ami noticed he looked beat. "You arrested her tonight, didn't you?"

"Yes."

"Did you arrest him, too?"

He tilted his head. "And you know how?"

"I swear I didn't question anyone. It hit me at the party tonight. They nodded to one another across the dance floor, and I saw it in their eyes. I just knew. How'd they take it?"

"Surprise, denial, anger. Eventually, she confessed to putting the potassium in the thermos, but not to murder."

"I don't understand."

"Claims their intent was to make Justin sick, not dead."

"Wow, didn't expect that. Did he confess?"

"No."

"Did she rat him out?"

"Yes."

"I assume her confession will make for an easier conviction."

"We also have plenty of evidence," assured Lucas.

"Yes, the DNA," emphasized Ami. "Do you have it on both of them?"

"Yes. What is it with you and DNA?"

"It's the insurance that keeps people from getting away with the crime."

"I'm talking about your obsession with it."

"I like to know it's there. It makes me feel more secure."

Lucas pulled her close and bundled her in a hug.

>=<

"That was such a delicious dinner!" complimented Marianne. "All my favorites!"

"Well, it's your birthday," said Josh. "We wanted to make it special for you."

"My favorite part was the dessert! Profiteroles are so much yummier than birthday cake."

"I thought you'd enjoy that, mon très cher," said Bill.

"Mary has prepared her famous espresso martinis as an after-dinner cocktail," announced Josh. "I'll get them while Bill settles you in the garden."

After Bill had seated everyone in comfortable chairs around the fire pit, Josh passed the tray of martinis, then, seated himself.

"Ooh, yummy," anticipated Marianne, taking a sip.

"Tasty, but problematic," warned Mike. "Marianne will be up all night talking."

"You can relax. The espresso is decaf," informed Josh.

"Doubt it will make a difference," shot Bill.

"Oh, give me a break. It's my birthday. Let's talk about something fun."

"It's your day; you choose the topic," invited Josh.

"Ooh, I know, I read about the arrest of Shelby Gibson and Roger Swanson and I want details, but, first, I want Uncle Lucas to tell me if I was right. Was it revenge?"

"It was a combination of jealousy and greed," blurted Bill.

"Bill! You should have let Lucas answer. It was his moment," scolded Josh.

Bill turned to Lucas. "My apologies."

"Please, take the floor with my blessing."

"Merci, mon bon homme."

"Come on, Bill, the details," urged Marianne, impatiently. "Why'd they do it?"

"Justin was a mutual obstacle. Shelby wanted to keep Justin from divorcing her so she wouldn't have to pay that hefty prenup penalty."

"She's the greed. What did Roger want?"

"Roger wanted Kathy Riggs back. He feared la relation amicale with Justin would turn into marriage after he divorced Shelby."

"And he'd lose his chance to win her back," finished Marianne. "He's the jealousy. Jealousy involves anger so I was right! It was revenge. They teamed up to take Justin's life."

Josh shook his head. "Not according to Shelby. She claims killing him was an accident. Roger miscalculated the amount of potassium he told her to give Justin. She'd been slipping it in his food for weeks."

"How was that an accident?" scoffed Marianne.

"She claims their plan was to give him a heart attack, not kill him."

"What would be the point in that?"

"Apparently, a recovering and infirm Justin would delay the divorce, allowing Shelby to talk him out of it. He'd be unable to see Kathy, allowing Roger the opportunity to win her back," explained Josh.

"Oh, what a laughable lie! A heart attack wouldn't stop him from divorcing Shelby or seeing Kathy."

"It's absurdité, incroyable! We don't believe it. Neither will a jury. Intent or not, Shelby's confession to putting the potassium in his food and in the thermos is enough to convict her."

"Shelby claims it was Roger's idea to set Roselyn up as a witness to filling Justin's thermos. The potassium had been added prior to her arrival," said Josh.

"What's Roger's side of all this?"

"Roger continues to deny any involvement," said Bill.

"But there's DNA," inserted Ami. "Roger's and Shelby's DNA were on the recovered potassium bottle and thermos. So, even though he denies involvement, Roger's DNA on both the thermos and potassium bottle prove he was involved."

"All I can say is they were pretty stupid not to wear gloves," said Marianne.

"Shelby said the items were wiped with a paper towel before disposing of them. It removed their fingerprints, but DNA doesn't wipe away that easy. They would have needed to use something like bleach to remove it," explained Ami.

"So between the DNA and Shelby's implicating him, Roger won't get away."

"No, he was the brains behind it," said Bill. "Shelby claims Roger chose the potassium, provided it to her and told her to slip the bottle into Justin's jacket to make it look like he was taking it on his own. Of course, neither Justin's fingerprints or DNA were on the bottle. Roger removed the thermos from the table while the EMTs were loading Justin in the ambulance and threw it in the trash behind the theater. It was meant to throw suspicion away from Shelby as an extra precaution should the potassium bottle in Justin's pocket not be believed."

"Oh, there's also the rehearsal video showing Roger watching Justin closely just before his heart attack," added Josh. "He was waiting for the potassium to kick in."

"The video shows Kathy and Will glancing over at Justin, too, but that was out of concern. They both had noticed his unsteady gate as he walked on stage. Has anyone talked with Kathy since the arrest?" asked Ami. "That must have been a terrible shock for her."

"I called her a couple times to check on her," said Josh. "Roger's involvement in Justin's death was her breaking point. She decided to go back home for good. Her friend, Allison, stepped in and volunteered to finalize everything for her, like the sale of her condo, car, furniture. Kathy packed a few boxes to ship and flew out last week."

"I can understand why she'd want to leave. She probably feels really guilty about Justin being killed," suggested Marianne.

"Why should she feel guilty?" asked Mike.

"Because it was her relationship with Justin that caused her ex-boyfriend to kill him."

"But she's not responsible for Roger's actions," protested Mike.

"Her feelings aren't logical right now, Mike, they're emotional. It's gonna be awhile before she gets her head straight and thinks clearly."

"Got it," replied Mike. He looked over at Ami and mouthed, "Hit a nerve."

She nodded affirmatively. Her eye caught Josh reach over and clasp Bill's hand and she noticed Bill had tears in his eyes. "What's wrong, Bill?"

"Les sentiments," answered Bill. "I was sure I'd feel better when Justin's killer was arrested, but now the excitement of the catch is fading, and I'm feeling the pain of losing him all over again."

"I'm sorry you're hurting, Bill."

"Thank you, mon cher ami."

"Let's talk about something more positive," suggested Marianne.

"Roselyn's getting all her jewelry back," offered Ami. "Clarence located the final two pieces."

"That's all to your credit," commended Lucas. "It was your investigation that uncovered Robby's scheme and aided his arrest."

"Thank you, but what pleases me most is Robby being punished for stealing from Roselyn and the others."

>=<

"Why don't you carry the tea tray into the living room, Mike," directed Claire. "I'll be right back."

Mike carried in the tray and set it on the coffee table.

"Granny having us for tea today means a lot to me. It reminds me of when I was a little girl. Granny gave me a tea party every year on my birthday. Mom, Aunt Ami and Shirley would join us. But, after I turned ten, Mom made her stop, saying I was too old."

Mike smiled at her. "Your mother can't stop this one."

"I have something special for you," said Claire, rejoining them and handing Marianne a box.

Marianne pulled off the ribbon, lifted off the top of the box and squealed. "Uncle Joe's mirror!"

"I thought you'd like it."

"But he left this to you. Don't you want to keep it?"

"I've enjoyed my time with it. Now, I think he'd want you to have it."

"Ooh, let's see what's in my future," intoned Marianne, gazing into the mirror.

"Are you going to let me in on this magic mirror?" asked Mike.

"My brother, Joe, started the mirror game when Suzy and Ami were little girls," explained Claire. "He'd ask them to gaze into it and tell him all about their future. Ami used to play along, but Suzy called it silly and refused.

171

When Shirley came along, he tried to play the mirror game with her, too.”

“Only Shirley was just like my mom and didn’t want to play either.”

“Talk about two peas in a pod. So, when Marianne came along, he was thrilled that she not only played along, but created elaborate stories. I remember how impressed he was with your imagination.”

“I remember feeling grateful he was listening to me. My parents usually dismissed my chattiness. I really can’t blame them. I talked non-stop.”

Mike nudged her. “Still do.”

“I know. Anyway, Uncle Joe listened to what I was saying and made me feel like my ideas were interesting. I loved him for that.”

“He loved you too, Darling,” assured Claire. “Now, you have a reminder of those happy memories.”

“Thank you, Granny. I’ll treasure this.”

>=<

Thank you for reading!

I hope you enjoyed book three in the Ami Dautry cozy mystery series and will join us again for a future adventure.

A KILLER OF A PORTRAIT
A SLASH OF COLOR
A NOTE TO DIE FOR